EVE'S BIG DECISION

THE AMISH QUILTING CIRCLE

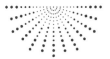

SARAH MILLER

IRENE GLICK

SWEETBOOKHUB.COM

WELCOME TO THE AMISH QUILTING CIRCLE

What is more lovely than a quilting circle? Where, good friends can come together to drink coffee, eat cake, talk, and work on a quilt or two. It is a wonderful way to spend an afternoon being both productive and having fun.

Only, this quilting circle likes to do a little matchmaking along with the quilting.

Join the ladies of Faith's Creek as they see who they will match next.

All the books are sweet and family-friendly with no nasty surprises.

If you missed the first book, you can grab An Englischer's Folly or the rest of the books here.

This book follows Eve's journey, we first met Eve in The Foundling in the Flowers, if you missed it grab it here.

If you are not already a member of my reader's newsletter, join here, for free, to be the first to find out when new books are released and for occasional free content.

CHAPTER ONE

ren't you beautiful? *Jah*, you are," Eve Lehman said, lifting her son, Esau, out of his Moses basket and cradling him in her arms.

He had been asleep for much of the afternoon and Eve had been busy working in the flower store alongside Annie, her cousin's new wife.

"He's been so *gut*, hasn't he? He's always *gut*. I've never known a *boppli* to sleep like him," Annie said, glancing up from the counter and smiling.

1

"He's getting bigger every day. I just look at him and... well, I can't believe he's mine," Eve said, smiling down at the *boppli*, who looked up at her and gurgled with delight.

It was a year since Eve had come to Faith's Creek on the greyhound bus from Philadelphia. She had been scared and confused, cradling Esau in her arms and not knowing what to do. Desperation had led her to the flower store, and she had left her *boppli* amongst the blooms, only for him to be discovered by Annie and taken care of. Those had been dark days, full of sorrow and Eve had been afraid of the future. But thanks to Annie's trust, and the help of Eve's cousin, Marshall, and her Aunt Linda, Marshall's *mamm*, all had come right. Once she admitted that she was his *mamm*, Eve had come to love Esau and cherish him.

"But he is yours, Eve. He's your flesh and blood, and he loves you, just as you love him," Annie replied, coming out from behind the counter and making her way heavily across the store floor.

She was with *kinner*, and the *boppli* was due imminently.

"Let me do that, Annie," Eve said, placing Esau back in his Moses basket, as Annie stooped to pick up an empty vase.

"It's all right. I won't be idle until it's necessary. I don't want to be treated like an invalid," Annie replied.

Eve smiled. She remembered when she was pregnant with Esau. It had been a difficult time, and now she was only too glad to help Annie in her pregnancy. The two had not quite worked out what to call their relationship – they were cousins-in-law, but they had become the closest of friends, too. Eve would be forever grateful to Annie for taking her *boppli* in and calling him Esau. The name suited him and she knew she owed Annie so much – and Marshall and her aunt – she owed them a debt of gratitude. They had taken her in, and when the truth about the *boppli* had been discovered, they had done all they could to help her. Eve had lived in Faith's Creek ever since, and now she truly felt a part of the community.

Her parents had been Amish, but they had rejected the way of life that Eve was now living. They had moved to Philadelphia when Eve was very young. Though they had remained Christian, their way of life had parted from the Amish. Now, bit by bit, and with the encouragement of Annie and Marshall, Eve was returning to the faith. She participated in prayer meetings and Bible studies and had begun to learn the *Ordnung*, hoping to eventually join the community her parents had rejected for her. Eve had been given *nee* choice in the matter, and the more she learned about the Amish way of life and saw the faith of those around her put into action, the more she longed to return to the way of life she should always have known.

"I know, but I just want to help you. I know what it's like to struggle through a pregnancy whilst still having to work. I worked all the hours I could at the restaurant in Philadelphia when I was carrying Esau, only for Mr. Harvey to let me go when I started showing too much. He said it would put the customers off their hamburgers. I told him the hamburgers at his crummy burger joint didn't need any help in putting people off. That was the last straw," Eve said, shaking her head as she thought back to the way of life she had known in Philadelphia.

Her life now was a total contrast to what she had lived before. In Faith's Creek, Eve was surrounded by a loving community and supported in raising Esau by Annie, Marshall, and her aunt. In Philadelphia, following the death of her parents, Eve had no one. She had struggled on her own, and Esau's *daed*, a man named Jack

Simmons, had wanted nothing to do with her once he found out she was pregnant.

She used to think she loved him and when he left she broke down a little. The strain was too much and that was how she ended up in Faith's Creek. Little did she know how much she would come to love it.

Sometimes she thought about Jack. She didn't even know if he knew she and Esau were living in Faith's Creek. But life was different now – far better than Eve had even imagined it could be when she had boarded the greyhound bus and set off into the unknown. Her parents had always talked disparagingly of the Amish, but in the community of Faith's Creek, Eve had found only kindness and charity and a new hope for the future.

"I can just hear you saying that," Annie said, laughing and shaking her head.

Eve blushed. "I'm not as outspoken now, I hope," she replied, not wishing Annie to think she had ever been deliberately rude.

But Eve's life had been filled with injustices – her sacking from the restaurant, her abandonment by Jack, and the premature death of her parents, had all contributed to making her life a tragedy, one from which she was only just beginning to recover.

"I hope you don't think my bouquets are crummy," Annie said, laughing, as she took stems of pink begonias from a vase and held them up to three orange lilies in her hand.

Eve shook her head. "I think they're all beautiful," she replied.

"*Gut*, because when I have this *boppli*, you'll be in charge here," Annie said.

Eve looked at her in surprise. They had not yet discussed the arrangements for the flower store, and she was honored to be asked to take it on, if only temporarily.

"Really? Are you sure?" she asked.

Annie nodded. "Sure as sure can be. There's no one else I'd trust but you. You've learned so much since coming to work here. You're ready to run the business, I know you are. I'll still be on hand, but I know I'll need a rest. Marshall's already insisted on it," Annie said.

The thought of such responsibility was daunting, but Eve reminded herself just how far she had come. She was no longer the naïve girl she once was. She was a *mamm*, and she had proved herself more than capable in such a role. Taking care of a *boppli* was not easy, but if Eve could do that, she could run a flower store, too.

"I won't let you down," she replied.

Annie smiled. "I know you won't. But come on, let's get these last few bouquets made up. We seem to have had a lot of anniversaries this month. April must be the time for weddings," Annie said, smiling at Eve, as she returned to the counter.

Esau started to cry, and Eve lifted him out of his Moses basket and kissed him on the forehead.

"I think you want attention, don't you?" she said, and the *boppli* gurgled and smiled at her.

"I'm surprised we haven't had one of the quilting circle ladies in here today. One of them usually finds an excuse to come in and see Esau. He's our best advertisement," Annie said, as she began to make up a bouquet with the orange lilies and begonias.

"I saw Sarah Beiler earlier when I took him out for some fresh air. She's been knitting for him. This *boppli* has more clothes than anyone I know," Eve said, cradling Esau in her arms.

"I think the whole community feels like he's somehow theirs," Annie replied.

Eve felt that, too. The community of Faith's Creek, and particularly the women of the quilting circle, had been instrumental in taking care of Esau following his appearance amongst the vases in the flower store. Eve knew there were still those who whispered as to her suitability as a *mamm*, but Annie always told her to ignore them. Eve had been through something terrible and she had made the best choices she could, and she was not to feel guilty for her past mistakes. What mattered was the future, and Eve hoped, in time, she would be accepted as a part of the community.

"You're right. And he is. He's got so many *grossmammis*," Eve said, laughing as the bell above the door jangled.

It was Sarah Beiler, and she had with her a bag of clothes, made by the ladies of the quilting circle, for Esau.

"We know he's growing so fast. But you can keep them for the next *boppli*," she said, handing over the bag to Eve, who had placed Esau back in his Moses basket.

"That's so kind of you, Sarah. *Denke*. I feel like I don't deserve all the help I'm getting," Eve said, feeling somewhat embarrassed.

In leaving Philadelphia, Eve had been determined to forge her own path, but she had learned the necessity of accepting kindness from others, and in the example of the Amish, she had come to know the truth about love and charity, stemming from a lively faith.

"We support one another, that's the Amish way," Sarah replied, smiling at Eve, before glancing into the Moses basket where Esau had now fallen asleep.

"I'm working hard on my *Ordnung*," Eve said.

"So I hear, Amos tells me you are doing well." Sarah smiled.

Eve was pleased with such praise from the bishop and his *fraa*. Studying did not come naturally to her, but with the help of her aunt, Eve was learning everything about the Bible and the set of rules governing the Amish way of life. Bishop Beiler had told her not to think of them as strict laws, but as a guide for living a better, simpler way of life. Having lived for so long outside the confines of an Amish community, Eve could see the benefits of a simpler, more *Gott*-centered way of life. She had grown tired of the hustle and bustle of Philadelphia, with its noisy streets and polluted air. Returning to Faith's Creek had been the greatest of blessings, and Eve was only too glad to immerse herself in the community she wanted to call her own.

"That's *gut*, Eve." Sarah smiled. "It's not a long document – if it's written down, but it takes time to make it a part of your own rhythm and rule. Every community has its variations, some don't write it down at all. Outsiders think it's oppressive, and that we live a strict and draconian life. But having rules and limits sets us free. That's what I've always found. We know our place in *Gott's* creation, and we live by a set of rules that help us make sense of the Bible and its teachings," the bishop's *fraa* said.

"I think I'll be ready to make a commitment soon. For Esau and me," Eve said.

Eve was not only doing this for herself. She wanted to raise Esau the right way, and she wanted him to grow up a part of the community, living by its values, and understanding its teachings. She agreed with Sarah Beiler's words – the *Ordnung* was not oppressive, it was liberating. In Philadelphia, she had known so many people who lived without a sense of purpose of direction. Their lives were a tragedy, and Eve had no desire to be like them. She wanted to feel a part of something, and to raise her son in a community of faith.

"Well, there's no rush. You can take your time. Keep studying the *Ordnung* and ask questions, too," Sarah said.

She bid them goodbye, promising another bag of clothes for Esau once he had outgrown the ones she had just given him. As the door closed, Eve smiled, turning to Annie, who looked up from the counter.

"Do you think I'm ready?" she asked.

"To make your commitment?" Annie replied.

Eve nodded, biting her lip as she waited for an answer. "I feel like it's time. You're all so kind. I want to be a part of that," Eve said.

Annie smiled at her. "I think you're close. But not everyone will," she said.

Eve sighed. She knew there were still some in the community who had no wish to see her return to the believers. She had to admit that she had endured whisperings and sideways glances ever since the truth as to her maternal relationship with Esau had been revealed.

"I know that, Annie. But I want to prove myself. I'm not the same person who got off that greyhound bus just over a year ago," Annie replied, and with *Gott's* help, she prayed the whole community would eventually come to realize that.

CHAPTER TWO

"Jonas? Jonas? Wake up, Jonas!" the voice in Jonas' ear demanded.

Jonas Byler opened his eyes, looking up in surprise at his brother, Henry, who stood over him, shaking his head.

"I... oh, did I fall asleep again?" he asked as he tried to clear his muddled and sleep-addled brain.

Henry nodded. "*Jah,* you did," he said, holding out his hand, and helping Jonas to his feet.

At twenty years old, Henry was two years younger than Jonas and possessed the family traits – ginger hair, and a dimpled chin. There were three brothers in the Byler household: Jonas, the eldest, Henry, and Levi, the youngest.

Jonas stifled a yawn. "Can you blame me? I've been up since four o'clock this morning. Levi was supposed to be helping. Where is he?" Jonas asked, looking around the farmyard, with an exasperated expression on his face.

"Where is he ever? He'll be off somewhere, doing precisely whatever he's not meant to be doing. You know what he's like. Come on, I'll help you with milking," Henry said.

Jonas had fallen asleep in the straw. This was the fifth morning in a row he had risen at such an early hour, and a full day of work was beckoning. The family ran a dairy farm on the edge of Faith's Creek, and their herd needed milking, come rain or shine. This task would have been made easier had the three brothers shared the responsibility equally. But Levi was always slacking and rarely did a day's work. Their *daed* was getting older and was unable to help as he had once done. The responsibility for running the farm now fell to Jonas, and he was finding it overwhelming.

"I should've finished hours ago. What time is it?" Jonas asked, glancing up at the sun, which was already climbing through the sky.

"Nearly nine o'clock. We'll get it done. You can't do everything, Jonas. Levi needs to pull his weight. Tell *daed* about it. Make him listen," Henry said, as the two men walked towards the milking parlor.

Jonas sighed. It was not that easy. Their *daed* doted on Levi as the youngest of the three, and there was always an excuse as to why the youngest brother could not pull his weight.

"You know he won't listen. Levi gets to do whatever Levi wants to do," Jonas replied, shaking his head.

They set about milking the cows. The dairy herd was large, and it was a job that took them several hours. Then there were the hens to see to, the feed to bring in, the fresh milk to transport... the list went on, and the work of the farm was never done.

"There, that's the last one – until tomorrow, at least," Henry said, straightening up, as the last of the cows left the barn.

Jonas mopped his brow. "There used to be four of us doing this, *Mamm*, too, if she came to help. We need farm hands, Henry. We need to employ someone," Jonas said.

Henry laughed, but it was not an amused sound, more a bark of defeat. "Try telling *Daed* that. Do you think he'll agree to employ someone when we're already running at a loss?" Jonas replied.

He had already tried making the suggestion to their *daed*, and it had fallen on deaf ears.

"But we're going to keep running at a loss. It's not going to get any better unless we make an investment. We do nothing with the milk except sell it at a loss to someone who makes a profit. That place that makes cheese – they're raking it in," Henry exclaimed.

Jonas nodded. He knew all the arguments. But their *daed* was stubborn and was determined to run the farm in the same way his own *daed* had run it before him. But times were changing, and whilst Jonas would never seek to abandon their traditional way of life, he knew it would not work unless the whole family pulled together.

"We're not going to change his mind about that. But we need to make Levi see the necessity of hard work. *Daed* isn't going to tell him, and he's not getting any younger, either. I don't know... it's all a mess, isn't it?" Jonas said, looking around him at the myriad of jobs that needed doing on the farm.

Roofs were leaking, fences needed repairing, and the hen coop was missing a part of its roof that had blown off in a storm. The farm was a disgrace, and Jonas felt ashamed to call it his own. He bore the heavy weight of responsibility, and he knew that responsibility would only increase as his *daed's* health grew worse, and Levi drifted further from his responsibilities. He was grateful to Henry for standing by him, but the two of them were exhausted, and things could not carry on as they were.

"It won't always be this way. But... well, it won't be easy. Then there's *Mamm*, too. I'm worried about her. Doctor Yoder didn't say much when he came, but... she's not well, Jonas. I heard her coughing all last night," Henry said.

Jonas had heard it, too. Their *mamm* has taken to her bed with a cold the previous week, and flu had soon set in. Faith's Creeks' resident physician, Doctor Yoder, had been summoned, but there had been little he could do except prescribe a tonic and tell Jonas and Henry to keep their *mamm* warm. Her condition was growing worse, and whilst she assured them she was getting better, it was clear she was not.

"I heard it, too. But... well, she doesn't like anyone fussing over her. Why don't you go and check on her? I need to go down to the mercantile for a few things. I won't be long," Jonas replied.

He would be glad of the walk, and set off across the farmyard, taking the track leading through the fields towards the cluster of houses around the market square. It was a bright, breezy, spring day, and the air was sweet with the scent of pollen. The last vestiges of winter had been blown away, replaced by the prospect of a long, hot summer to come. This was Jonas' favorite time of year, a time of potential and new beginnings. But in his heart, he felt despondent. The farm was failing, his family was fractured, and between working all hours and supporting his parents, Jonas had little time for himself. He was twenty-two years old and had lived his whole life in Faith's Creek. The demands of the farm had prevented him from ever setting out on a *rumspringa*, and now it seemed his life was to take a downward course, as he navigated the end of a farming legacy stretching back several generations.

"I wish I could be carefree like Levi," he thought to himself. What would it be like to do nothing? Could he change his life, could he start afresh, and if so what would that do to the family?

CHAPTER THREE

As Jonas made the walk he thought about Levi. No doubt, his youngest brother would be in Bird-in-Hand, or off with his friends. He cared nothing for responsibility, and their *daed* indulged him far too readily. Whilst Jonas and Henry were expected to see to every job on the farm, Levi would sleep late, helping when he felt like it – which was rare. He never offered to assist or put himself out. He lived for himself, and Jonas was growing to resent him.

"But he won't listen to me," Jonas said to himself, as he came in sight of the market square.

It was market day, and the stalls were busy. Jonas needed a new hammer shaft – the head had flown off his old one the day before, narrowly missing a window of the house – and he had it in mind to buy the materials to repair the chicken coop roof. But Jonas's chief reason for walking to the store that morning was escape. He was going mad on the farm, and it was no wonder Henry had found him fast asleep in the hay that morning. The expectations placed on him were too great, and Jonas knew he could not continue as he was, without a drastic change. But what could that change be?

"*Gut* morning, Jonas. What can I do you for?" Marshall Lehman, one of the counter clerks, asked, as Jonas entered the store a few moments later.

"I need a new hammer shaft, and some felt roof tiles, the black ones," Jonas said, pointing to the wall of tools behind the counter.

Jonas liked the store. It had a particular smell to it – wood polish and timber chippings. Marshall nodded, taking down a shaft and placing it on the counter.

"How are things up at the farm?" he asked, turning to retrieve the roof tiles Jonas had indicated.

"Well... if you happen to see my brother, tell him he might like to come and do some work today – or even this week," Jonas replied.

He had long since tired of defending Levi or making excuses for him. His brother was growing increasingly into a lost cause, and if he did not change his ways, Jonas feared he would ever stray from the path he and Henry now walked.

"I haven't seen him in a month. You should hire someone. Plenty of young men are looking for work," Marshall said, as he rang up the cash register.

"My *daed* won't hear of it. We've always managed with what we've got. That's his motto," Jonas replied, handing over the payment.

"Times change though, don't they? You can't run that farm single-handedly, not if your brother won't pull his weight," Marshall said, shaking his head.

Jonas thanked him for the advice. But no amount of persuasion could change his *daed's* mind. Atlee Byler was a stubborn man, who still thought he had the strength of one half his age. He was forever talking about getting back to work, but his strength had failed him in the past few years, and he was incapable of early rising or putting in a full day's work. Jonas could not blame his *daed* for that. He was in his sixties, the three brothers having been born late, and he simply could not manage the demands of a dairy herd and farm. Jonas would gladly have accepted this, save for the fact that his *daed* refused to make Levi pull his weight or hire others to help.

And that's not going to change, he thought to himself, emerging from the store and crossing the square toward the flower store.

Jonas's *mamm* loved flowers, and he had it in mind to purchase a bouquet to cheer her up. The bell above the flower store door jangled as he entered, and the air was filled with the sweet and heady scent of the blooms.

"*Gut* morning," the proprietress, Annie Lehman, the *fraa* of Marshall, said, smiling at Jonas as he looked around him.

"I'd like some roses, please. The yellow ones," he said, pointing to a vase of tall stems in bloom.

At that moment, the cry of a *boppli* filled the air, and Jonas was surprised to see a young woman rush out from the storeroom behind the counter and pick up a *boppli* from a Moses basket placed amongst the vases.

"Don't mind me, I'm just seeing to the *boppli*," she said when she noticed him staring.

She was very pretty, with a touch of brown hair escaping her *kapp* and bright blue eyes. Muttering sweet nothings, she cradled the *boppli* in her arms, shushing him, as Annie arranged the bouquet.

"I'm sorry if Esau startled you," she said.

Jonas recalled hearing about a woman named Eve who was Marshall's cousin and had come to Faith's Creek from Philadelphia. The rumor had it that she had abandoned the *boppli* amongst the vases in the flower store.

All that had happened a year ago, and Eve was now about to be received into the community. He had seen her a couple of times from a distance, but this was the first time he had found himself in her company.

"Oh... it's all right. He's got a healthy pair of lungs on him," Jonas replied, as Eve shushed the *kinner* in her arms.

She glanced at him and smiled. "He certainly has," she replied, but before Jonas could reply, Eve gave a cry of exclamation.

Annie looked up from the counter in surprise.

"What's wrong?" she asked, but Eve shook her head, even as her expression suggested something was terribly wrong.

"It's all right... it's nothing," she replied, as Annie handed over the flowers.

Jonas was confused, but he said nothing, paying for the bouquet and wishing them a *gut* day. But as he left the store, he was surprised to see a man standing on the far side of the market square, staring through the window intently, and as he looked back, Jonas could see the fear on Eve's face as she cradled Esau in her arms. Was this man up to *nee gut*?

CHAPTER FOUR

Eve *had* been surprised at the sight she had seen through the window of the flower store, and as the handsome young man left with his bouquet of yellow roses, she turned to Annie filled with fear.

"What's wrong?" Annie repeated as Eve glanced fearfully over her shoulder.

"I've seen someone... not just anyone... oh, it's... it can't be. I must be mistaken," she exclaimed.

Annie took hold of her by the arms even as she held Esau close. Her heart was racing, for she was terrified by what she had seen, even as she could barely believe it to be true.

"What is it?" Annie asked, looking thoroughly confused.

"It's... I think it's Jack," Eve replied, glancing again out of the window at the figure standing on the far side of the market square.

Jack Simmons was Esau's *daed*, but Eve had heard nothing from him since she had fled to Faith's Creek. She had not even realized he knew where she was. He had left as soon as he found out she was pregnant and he had made no attempt to find out where she had gone. She never expected to see him again, let alone expected him to come and find her here. He had wanted nothing to do with Eve when she had discovered she was pregnant, and despite her best efforts to make him understand the enormity of this new responsibility, he had simply washed his hands of her.

"Jack? Esau's *daed*? But he can't be here," Annie said, crossing to the window and peering out from behind the vases of flowers.

"I can't be certain but... he's watching the store. It looks like him. He's tall, isn't he, with black hair, and he'll be wearing jeans, he always wore jeans," Eve said.

Annie turned to her and nodded. "If it's him, he matches your description. I've never seen him before. He's not from Faith's Creek," Annie said.

Eve looked down at Esau, who had fallen asleep in her arms. The thought of Jack's return filled her with dread. What did he want?

"It's him. It's got to be him. Oh... I don't know what to do, Annie. I can't hide in here forever. He'll come and find me." Eve didn't know what to think but she was afraid. She knew that his being here couldn't be *gut*.

The timing was awful too, she had only just settled into life in Faith's Creek and life as a new *mamm*. It had taken her time to find her feet in a new community. Jack's arrival brought disruption. It was a reminder of a past she wanted to forget, a past she had hoped would not catch up with her.

"Is he dangerous? What does he want? I could go and fetch Marshall," Annie said, still peering out from behind the vases of flowers.

Eve knew Jack was not dangerous, indifference was his failing. She simply could not understand why he would want anything to do with her and Esau, now. He had been given a chance, and he had not taken it. Eve had wanted Jack to be a *daed* to Esau, but he had refused, leaving her heartbroken. It had taken time to recover and she didn't feel that he deserved a way back into her life, or that of her son.

"He's not dangerous, *nee*. He'd never harm me or the *boppli*. But... oh, I'll have to go and speak to him. If he's come all this way, he's not going to just disappear, is he?" she said, shaking her head.

"I'll come with you if you want me to," Annie said.

But Eve knew she had to face Jack alone. She would find out why he had come here and ask him what he expected of her. This was something she had to do alone, and taking a deep breath, she held Esau out to her cousin-in-law.

"*Nee*, it's all right. You take care of Esau. I'll go," she said, summoning all her courage.

She had barely given Jack a second thought since she had come to terms with his betrayal. He represented a very different world, one she would rather forget. The two had met in Philadelphia. He had told her he loved her, and when she had discovered she was pregnant, it had seemed like the happiest of times. But Eve's excitement at the prospect of being a *mamm* had soon given way to sadness at the realization of Jack's distancing himself. He had not wanted to be a *daed*, and reluctantly, Eve had given up trying to make him be one. She couldn't hold onto him and he had left her to deal with the birth alone. Once she lost her job, she almost had a breakdown and that was how she ended up here.

"Be careful, Eve. We don't know why he's come back," Annie said, taking Esau in her arms and holding him close.

"Perhaps he wants to be a part of Esau's life. I wouldn't begrudge him that. But I'll be careful, I promise," Eve said.

Despite her initial shock and fear, Eve was curious as to why Jack had come all this way to find her. It felt strange to think of him having tracked her down, and despite her reticence, a part of her still felt something of those old feelings they had shared. Eve had been in love with Jack, and he had told her he loved her, too. Had he come to rekindle something she had thought lost?

"I only need to talk to him, that's all," she said to herself, checking her *kapp* in a mirror by the door.

Eve was not obliged to wear a *kapp*. But she had taken to doing so in recent weeks, eager to prove her commitment to the way of life she intended to embrace formally very soon. It still felt and looked strange, for she had spent a lifetime without it. To Annie and the other women, such garments were a natural addition. They hardly thought about them. But the act of putting on her *kapp* still felt different. Eve had never covered her hair before coming here, and whilst she knew many outside the community would view it as an act of subjugation, to Eve, modesty in dress was as natural as modesty in speech and action. She liked wearing the *kapp*. It gave her a sense of belonging, and she was proud of what it represented. In Philadelphia, Eve had felt lost in the crowd, but here, in Faith's Creek, she had found her purpose and sense of belonging.

"I'll be waiting for you here. Take as much time as you need. But don't let him manipulate you, Eve. Men are *gut* at that. Having a *boppli* was your choice, and we're all glad of it... but he abandoned you so he has *nee* hold over you," Annie said.

Eve glanced back at her cousin-in-law and smiled. "I won't, I promise. I'm just going to talk to him, that's all," she replied, taking a deep breath as she pulled open the door.

The bell above it jangled, and the hustle and bustle of the market square greeted her. Monica Hertz was serving customers on her wool stall, and she looked up at Eve and smiled.

"It's busy today, isn't it? I don't know where everyone's come from," she said, shaking her head.

"It's *gut* for business," Eve said, distracted, as she looked across the market square to where Jack was standing looking at her.

As she got closer, there was *nee* doubt it was him. He looked *nee* different, though it had only been a year and a half since last she had seen him. If it had not been for the past they shared, she might still have found him attractive. His black hair was combed to one side, his jeans fashionably ripped, and his well-built physique stood out against the crowd of simply dressed Amish men and women going about their day.

"It certainly is. Sometimes I wonder why I bother running a stall like this. But on a fresh spring day, when the sun shines, I remember why," Monica continued.

Eve nodded, not entirely paying attention to the stall-holder. Her heart was beating fast at the thought of what was to come. She was uncertain how to approach her former partner, the man she had intended to marry. She had assumed he would come to meet her. But he remained standing on the far side of the square, still watching her intently. It made her feel uncomfortable, even as the voice at her side brought her back to her senses.

"Haven't you got the *boppli* with you today?" Eve turned to find Alima Byler, a woman with whom she had already had unpleasant dealings, standing with another woman, watching her intently.

Alima was a troublemaker, and she could be mean. She had been amongst Eve's most vocal opponents, and whilst she was civil to her face, Eve knew she was often whispering behind her back. The fact of the matter was made worse by her being distantly related to Bishop Beiler and his *fraa*, Sarah, both of whom could not have been kinder to Eve in the aftermath of her arrival in Faith's Creek. Alima was the sort of woman who went to church on Sunday and forgot the sermon by Monday morning. She displayed a holier-than-thou attitude, whilst forgetting that fundamental Christian tenet: love thy neighbor as thyself.

"He's with my cousin-in-law," Eve replied.

She had no time for Alima that day, and whilst she would never dream of being rude – that would only serve as further ammunition for her detractor – Eve was not about to enter into an argument.

"I'm surprised you come to work with a *boppli* in tow. It's no place for a *boppli*, a flower store," Alima continued, and the woman standing next to her nodded.

"All that pollen in the air. It can't be *gut* for the lungs," she said.

Eve turned to them and drew herself up, fixing them with a hard stare. "I think a *mamm* knows what's best for her *boppli*, don't you?" she replied.

The two women glanced at one another. "I suppose pollen might be marginally better than traffic fumes – that's what you'd have got if you'd stayed in Philadelphia," Alima said, turning her nose up.

Eve rolled her eyes. There was no point in arguing with her. She had made up her mind as to Eve's fall from grace. In Alima's eyes, there could be no redemption – only perpetual punishment for past sins. She chose to ignore the more difficult parts of the Bible concerning forgiveness, and whether Eve had turned over a new leaf or not, it seemed Alima was determined to judge her and find fault.

"Then I'll choose pollen... if you'll excuse me," Eve said, walking purposefully off across the square.

"She's not fit to be a *mamm*, and if she thinks a *kapp* makes a difference, she's sorely mistaken," Alima said, loud enough for Eve to hear.

But remembering all she had learned about forgiveness and Christian charity, Eve bit her lip. She had more important things to think about, and now she approached Jack, her heart beating, as she wondered why he had come to see her...

CHAPTER FIVE

As Eve approached, Jack looked at her and smiled. He had not changed a bit, and Eve wondered what he would think of her, dressed in a simple blue dress, white apron, and wearing a shawl around her shoulders. In days gone by, Eve had dressed like any other young person in Philadelphia, favoring an immodesty she could only imagine her aunt's face if she saw. But those days were gone, and Eve had chosen a different path to take.

"I thought it was you," Jack said.

Eve returned his smile.

He had a way of charming her with a look, and now she remembered the first time they had met. She had been working at the restaurant, and Jack had come in with some friends to order milkshakes. He had been watching her the whole evening, with an intensity that made her feel wanted. When they spoke he looked deep into her eyes and told her she was beautiful, and as he left, he asked for her number. She had been shy at first, telling him she did not usually give her number to strangers. He had gone away, but the next evening he had come to the restaurant alone, telling her he would come every day until she could no longer call him a stranger. It had worked, and Eve had given him her number.

It had not taken her long to fall in love with him, she was caught up in the romance they enjoyed. He took her to parties, to the mall, and to the bowling alley. They shared milkshakes at the restaurant, and he bought her little gifts. Flowers, trinkets, just things to make her smile. Jack introduced her to his friends. It had all seemed so perfect, until the day she discovered she was pregnant with Esau.

"You haven't changed," Eve replied, looking up at him shyly.

"But you have. What is this place? I've never been to an Amish community before. It's all so... quaint. And you, too. Dressed like that. You're not... one of them, are you?" he asked with a smirk on his handsome face.

Eve looked at him in surprise and felt a touch of annoyance. She had made no secret of her family's past. He had known she was Amish, at least by birth.

"I live here with my aunt and cousin and his *fraa*... wife. I'm learning the *Ordnung* and Bible study, too. I'm committed to the community," she said, even as he raised his eyebrows.

"You're going back to this? Why?" he asked, shaking his head in astonishment.

Eve had not expected such a challenge, and she faltered, uncertain of what to say. To her, it seemed obvious why, and yet she found it hard to put into words. This was her tradition. It was where she belonged. It felt right and safe and her future was exciting here and scary. Her parents should never have taken her to Philadelphia, and Eve found herself feeling resentful as to Jack's question.

"I'm not going back to anything. It's where I belong," she replied, feeling hurt by the dismissive manner in which he surveyed the surrounding scene.

He shook his head, furrowing his brow, as though he could not understand why anyone would swap life in Philadelphia for that of Faith's Creek.

"Look, I understand why you left, and I've come to say I'm sorry for what happened," he said.

"Sorry? Is that right? And what about that woman you went off with. Did she get bored of you? Is that it? Is that why you came to find me?" Eve asked.

Her defenses were raised, and her suspicions heightened. After she had revealed she was with *kinner*, Jack had grown distant. After he left her, she had caught him with another woman, sharing a milkshake in the very restaurant where she worked and they had first met. Louise McCartney was her name – she was pretty, vivacious, and did not come with a *boppli* in tow. Jack had made his decision, and Eve had believed they had gone their separate ways, a line drawn under their past relationship. Jack was Esau's *daed*, and Eve accepted that, but as for accepting his apology...

"Look, can we go and talk? There's a café over there. Let's get something to eat. I've been on the greyhound bus for what feels like a month. I need a proper meal," Jack said.

Eve nodded. There was no point in being churlish. He had come to Faith's Creek to say something to her, and it would be wrong not to hear what it was he had to say.

And as for forgiveness, you know what Bishop Beiler told you, Eve thought.

Forgiveness was something she found difficult, despite knowing it was her Christian duty to do so. The Bible taught absolute forgiveness. How many times to forgive those who wrong you? Seven times, no seventy-seven times seven – always. But Eve would find it difficult to forgive Jack for abandoning her in her hour of need. Had he come to beg or to gloat? She thought of Esau. He was the most precious gift she had ever received, a gift from *Gott,* and a gift from Jack. He was Esau's *daed,* and she owed as much to hear his explanation, whatever it might be.

"I can take half an hour. I'll need to get back to Esau. I've asked my cousin-in-law to look after him," Eve said, as together they made their way towards *The Seymour Café,* a pine-clad diner, serving Amish food and strong coffee.

"How's he doing? Esau, I mean? I didn't realize he was called that. It's a nice name" Jack said, as they entered the diner.

"He's a happy little boy," Eve said.

This was the truth, though she saw no need to tell Jack about the circumstances following her arrival in Faith's Creek. If Jack knew she had abandoned the *boppli* in the flower store, he might seek to challenge her for custody. The thought gripped her with sudden fear, and she drew a sharp intake of breath.

"And?" he asked, looking at her pointedly.

To Eve's relief, a waitress came up to them, smiling and ushering them to a table for two.

"We've got a special on today – apple and cinnamon fritters with sour cream," she said.

"Is that what they eat around here?" Jack asked.

"Two portions, please, and a pot of coffee," Eve replied.

She remembered Jack's liking for burgers and deep-pan pizza, but he would struggle to find such things in Faith's Creek, where the population preferred the likes of buttered noodles and chuck steak casserole.

"It's a different world here, isn't it? Are you really happy?" Jack asked.

Eve fixed him with a searching gaze. "What brought you here? I don't understand," she said.

The look in his eyes worried her, was he here to cause trouble? Did he want to be part of his son's life, and if he did, what would she do?

CHAPTER SIX

Jack sighed, arching his fingers together and resting his chin on the point. "I wanted to see you. I wanted to see the baby too; I hear you have called him Esau," he replied.

This was what caused Eve the most worry, even as she had known Jack would ask to see the *boppli* – he was Esau's *daed*, and surely had a right to do so. But Esau knew nothing of his *daed*, and whilst he was only a year old, Eve felt uncertain about Jack bursting suddenly onto the scene and taking on the paternity he had previously walked away from. This could be very confusing for her son and it was worrying for her. *What were Jack's real motives? Why was he here?*

He was looking at her and she could see a touch of annoyance crossing his features. Maybe, she was best to go along with this and hope that he would soon leave. "Well..." The word's stuck in her throat. She couldn't say it, she wanted him gone despite the old infatuation telling her he was a *gut* man.

"I've come all the way from Philadelphia, Eve. Are you really going to deny me the chance to see my own son?" he asked.

Eve could not deny him that, but she remained wary of his motives. "You weren't in a hurry to see him before," she said, knowing her words were cutting, but wanting Jack to understand the heartache he had put her through.

"I was confused. I... didn't think I wanted him, but... it's different now," he replied.

Eve wondered *how* it was different. The last time she had seen him, he had told her he wanted nothing to do with the *boppli* and that he was happy with his new beau.

"How's Louise?" she asked, as the waitress set the apple and cinnamon fritters down on the table.

"I'll bring your sour cream with the coffee," she said, bustling away.

Jack looked confused. "Louise?" he asked, with a puzzled expression.

"The woman you left me for. *That* Louise," Eve replied, with a note of exasperation in her voice.

"Oh... she's long gone," he replied.

Eve rolled her eyes. This was Jack's problem. He was a serial womanizer. There had probably been a string of women since Louise, and the only reason he was here now was that his relationship with Eve had resulted in an unplanned arrival. A permanence he couldn't shake... but he had, so why was he back?

"You got bored with her, did you?" Eve asked.

There had been a time when she wanted only to please Jack – to make him like her at any cost, so that he would stay with her. But those days were long gone, and she was only too willing to speak her mind.

He looked at her and sighed. "Look, Eve, I came here because... well, I realized my responsibilities. I shouldn't ever have treated you like I did. It was wrong, and I'm sorry," he said.

Eve's heart softened a little. He had a way of apologizing for his wrongs, with a hang-dog look on his face, as though butter would not melt in his mouth.

"No, you shouldn't have," she replied, as the waitress set down the pot of coffee and a pot of sour cream.

"Let me know if I can get you anything else," she said, smiling at them.

Eve nodded her gratitude.

Jack poured himself a cup of coffee, and Eve took up her fork, wondering what was coming next. It was not like Jack to apologize for anything, and whilst forgiveness remained difficult, Eve could at least be grateful for the attempt he was making at reconciliation. To come all the way from Philadelphia gave a sincerity to his words, and Eve was at least willing to listen to his explanation.

"And that's why I want to make amends. Isn't forgiveness a part of all this?" he asked her, waving his fork in a large circle before digging it into one of the fritters.

Eve had to admit it was. Since beginning to study the *Ordnung* and the faith, she had come to realize just how radical the call to conversion could be. Forgiveness and the renunciation of worldly vices meant some hard acceptances. It was one thing to show love to those who returned love, but to love the sinner, to forgive those who did you wrong, and to step back from a world of materialism and greed, replacing it with the simplicities of a life lived not for oneself but for *Gott* – these things were radical, and in accepting the call to repent, Eve had been forced to make sacrifices of her past feelings. She *had* to forgive Jack, but more than that, she had to want to forgive him.

"It is, but how do I know you're sincere?" she asked, fixing him with a searching gaze.

He chewed his apple fritter ponderously, a smile coming over his face.

"Would I really have come here if I wasn't? I could've stayed in Philadelphia and carried on as though nothing had happened. But something pricked my conscience. You might call it divine intervention, I don't, but here we are. I shouldn't have washed my hands of you and... Esau. It was wrong, and I realize that now. I want to make amends. I want to be a good father to him," Jack replied.

The implications of this were clear, and Eve wondered how Jack intended to be a good *daed* to Esau when they were separated by a difficult journey of many hours. Did Jack intend to move to Faith's Creek in order to be near their son? If so, did she want this? Was there a chance for them, after all? She pushed that thought away. He had wheedled his way back into her life one too many times.

"I admire you for realizing your duties," she replied.

Jack smiled at her. "Then I can see him?" he asked.

Eve could not deny a *daed* the chance to see his son. To do so would be cruel, and she was not a cruel person. Reluctantly, she nodded.

"You can see him. I won't deny you that. But I don't understand how you hope to be a *daed* to him? Aren't you going back to Philadelphia soon?" she asked.

He took another forkful of fritter before answering, sitting back with a sigh. "It's different food here, isn't it?" he said, laying aside his fork, and pushing his plate aside.

"It's a little different from takeaway burgers and deep-pan pizzas. At least here, it's honest food, all cooked from scratch. But you're not answering the question. How can you be a *daed* to him if you live so far away?" she asked.

He smiled at her. "You even use their words – "daed" – it's strange to hear you speak like that. It doesn't matter how I'll do it. We'll come to that later. But can I see him? I've been thinking about seeing him for so long," Jack said, looking at Eve with a hopeful expression on his face.

She smiled and nodded, won over, as ever, by his charm. "All right, are you paying the bill?" she asked, finishing the last of her apple fritters and praying she was doing the right thing.

He nodded and smiled. What she had to decide was if it was the smile of a friend or one to lull her into the jaws of a shark.

CHAPTER SEVEN

The flowers were very pretty. Annie had done them up with a bow and ribbon, wrapping them in brown paper, and Jonas was looking forward to giving them to his *mamm*. At the very least, they would cheer her up. She had been so miserable lately – stuck in bed, when she was used to being up and about, taking care of the house and looking after three sons and a husband. Jonas was glad to be doing something nice for her, and as he approached the farmhouse, he pictured the look on her face as he presented her with the bouquet.

She'll be pleased with them, I know she will, he thought to himself, trying not to think about the dozens of jobs waiting to be done around the farm.

He was pleased with the flowers, and his thoughts returned to the pretty young assistant cradling her *boppli*. He was curious about her and had heard *gut* and bad sides to her story. Abandoning a *boppli* was a serious business, but it was clear she had tried to make amends for her actions and was now doing all she could to take care of the *kinner*.

"She'll love those," Henry said, emerging onto the porch from the house as Jonas came up the steps.

"I hope so. They might cheer her up a bit," Jonas replied, setting down the bag from the mercantile and pulling off his boots.

"They're bound to cheer her up more than her visitor is," Henry said, raising his eyebrows.

Jonas looked at his brother in surprise. "Visitor? What visitor? I thought Doctor Yoder said she needed rest," he replied.

"Aunt Alima's here," Henry replied, striding off across the farmyard.

Jonas groaned. He knew well enough why his brother was making himself scarce. Their Aunt Alima was trouble, and she brought strife wherever she went. She was their *daed's* sister, an unmarried woman who made it her business to interfere in the affairs of others and offer her opinion where it was not wanted. A visit from Aunt Alima meant an afternoon of hearing your faults and the faults of others. She rarely had a nice word to say about anyone, and when she did, it would come with a poison twist.

I might hide in the barn, Jonas thought to himself, but knowing his *mamm* was suffering the fate of the visit alone, he bravely made his way inside.

"You tell Doctor Yoder it's not *gut* enough. He's useless, he really is. He doesn't prescribe anything but tonics, and what *gut* are they?" – Jonas could hear her voice echoing down from his *mamm's* bedroom on the landing above the parlor.

He steeled himself for what was coming, knowing he would not escape the criticism of his aunt, who always had an opinion on the goings on at the farm. The parlor was messy, and the kitchen worktops were piled high with dirty dishes. The house was in disarray, but Jonas had simply not had time to do anything but see to the farm and keep the family business going. His *daed* was nowhere to be seen, and now Jonas made his way upstairs, pausing in the doorway of his *mamm's* bedroom, as his aunt was still in full flow. His *mamm* looked up at him with relief. She was an elderly woman, her graying hair covered by her *kapp*, and the lines on her face more prominent than ever. She looked tired and weaker than he had hoped, she was wrapped in blankets, lying on the bed.

"Oh, there you are, Jonas. How lovely to see you," she said, as his aunt looked up, her eyes narrowing.

She had a cruel face, as well as a cruel disposition, and always carried a pocket Bible, ready to quote scripture at the drop of a hat. She was sitting close to the bed, wearing the normal, plain cotton dress, with a blue shawl wrapped around her shoulders, her spectacles resting on the tip of her nose.

"I brought you some flowers, *Mamm*. I thought they might cheer the place up a bit," he said, stepping into the room.

"Yellow roses? My favorite," his *mamm* exclaimed, a smile breaking over her face.

She had a beautiful smile, and it gladdened Jonas to see it. She would get better, Doctor Yoder had assured them of that, but to see her so weak and helpless broke his heart.

"How are you feeling?" Jonas asked, pulling up a chair to sit next to the bed.

"A little better. Henry brought me some soup earlier on, and your *daed's* gone out to get me an iced bun from the Millers' bakery. It's just what I fancy to eat, and they are doing those delicious ones with the maple syrup cream," she said.

Jonas smiled. "I'm glad he's doing something."

"And what's that supposed to mean?" his aunt asked.

Jonas looked at her. He did not want to argue, but Aunt Alima delighted in doing so, and she was always quick to jump to conclusions.

"Nothing, I didn't mean anything by it. It's just... well, we could do with some help on the farm, that's all," he said.

"And you're saying your *daed* doesn't help you?" Aunt Alima replied huffing a little as she did.

"I'm not saying that at all. But there's a lot to do. I went to the store today and bought new felt tiles for the chicken coop. I'll repair it when I've got the time. But I'd be glad of *daed's* help doing so." Jonas realized he had stepped on a mine and was trying to get off it safely.

There *were* jobs his *daed* could do, even if much of the work around the farm was beyond him now. It was as though he had given up on his own ambitions, even as he still expected the farm to run as it once had.

"Where did you get the flowers from, Jonas? They're beautiful, and what a delightful scent," his *mamm* said, clearly sensing the beginnings of an argument.

"From the flower store on the market square. They've got so many beautiful blooms, and..." Jonas began, but his aunt interrupted.

"You went *there*?" she exclaimed.

Jonas looked up at her in surprise. Surely, she could not find fault with the flower store run by the pleasant and delightful wife of Marshall Lehman.

"I did. Why, what's the problem?" he asked as she glared daggers at him. A sigh escaped for he thought he knew the problem and he realized that he had stepped off the mine into a steaming pile of farmyard manure.

CHAPTER EIGHT

"You should stay away from that place," Alima exclaimed, the look in her eye one of disgust.

Jonas could not understand his aunt's attitude. She was a Pharisee, always quoting rules, and expecting others to live up to her own apparent perfection. But her judgment of others was wrong, and Bishop Beiler had warned her about it on several occasions.

"Why?" he asked, knowing that he was pushing her and that it would have been better to just agree.

"*She* works there. The *Englischer* girl, the one from Philadelphia who had a *boppli* out of wedlock. The one who abandoned said *boppli* amongst the flowers and expected the rest of the community to take care of it. She's a disgrace. You shouldn't have anything to do with her, Jonas, *nee* decent man should."

Jonas sighed. He had known his aunt would have an opinion on the matter. He thought back to his brief encounter with the pretty young assistant cradling the *boppli* in her arms. She had made a mistake in abandoning it, but it was clear she had made amends. Jonas had seen her in the square later on, talking to a man – an *Englischer* by the looks of it. But there was nothing out of place about Eve. She had been wearing a *kapp*, and her modest dress suggested she was trying her best to become a part of the community in which she now lived. Driving her away would be terribly wrong, and it pained Jonas to hear his aunt speak with such venom in her voice.

"Is that so? Well, shouldn't we be glad she's back with the *boppli* and taking care of it?" he asked.

His aunt scowled. "That's what happens when outsiders arrive. We've had too much of that lately. They bring their big city ideas here, and then what happens... *nee*, you mark my words, she's trouble, that one. A *boppli* needs a *mamm* and a *daed*," Aunt Alima said.

"Not every family's perfect, you know. We've got our problems, too," Jonas said.

"And what do you mean by that? I don't see any unmarried *mamms* in this house," his aunt said, as Jonas's *mamm* sat between them in the bed, looking thoroughly uncomfortable.

"If she's turned over a new leaf..." she ventured, but she was shouted down by Aunt Alima.

"Leopards don't change their spots. She came here because she thought she'd get an easy ride of it. And she has – Marshall and Annie are at her beck and call, and so is Linda, her aunt. She should go back to Philadelphia. She's not welcome here," Alima replied, folding her arms.

"How can you say that? You don't know her. I found her... charming," Jonas replied.

He was growing angry now, his resentment towards his *daed* and brother was boiling over, and his aunt's words only served to further anger him. She knew nothing about Eve – no one did. She had come to Faith's Creek because she was desperate for help, and she had found that help in the goodness and charity of many of those whom she had encountered. That was the story Jonas had heard – the opposite of the cruel and heartless words of his aunt.

"I'm sure she is. But don't be fooled. Those sorts of women are all the same," Aunt Alima said.

Jonas was about to respond when footsteps on the stairs caused him to look up. Levi was standing in the doorway, looking as though butter would not melt in his mouth.

"Can I get you anything, *Mamm*? A pot of coffee, perhaps, or a piece of shoofly pie. There's some leftover from dessert last night," he said.

"Oh, it's all right, dear. *Denke*, your *daed's* gone down to the bakery for me," she replied, smiling at Levi, who nodded.

"If you need anything – anything at all – just ask," he said.

Jonas grimaced. It was just like his brother to behave in such a way. Their *mamm* knew nothing of his faults – his laziness, irresponsibility, and refusal to do anything resembling work. Their *daed* appeased him and would hear no criticism of his favorite son.

"You could help me with the chicken coop, Levi. I need someone to hold the roof tiles in place whilst I hammer them in securely," Jonas said.

He knew his words would be met with an excuse, but he wanted to challenge his brother. Things could not continue as they were, and if Levi was not willing to pull his weight, there would have to be consequences. His brother sighed, feigning a mock look of disappointment.

"Oh... I'm sorry, Levi. I can't help you. I'm feeling really tired today. I didn't sleep well last night. I hope I'm not coming down with the same fever as *Mamm*," he said, coughing pathetically as he spoke.

"He works too hard, that boy. I've said it before, Mary," Aunt Alima said, tutting and shaking her head.

"I don't want to worry you, *Mamm*. I'm sure I'll be all right. I'll help with the chicken coop as soon as I'm feeling better," he said, fixing Jonas with a look that challenged him to object.

"I'll wait until you are. We won't have eggs if the hens aren't dry. They won't lay on damp straw," Jonas replied.

He was beginning not to care – the farm could go to rack and ruin, then they would be sorry. If Jonas and Henry stopped doing the work of ten men as they were now, the family would quickly slide into destitution, and yet no one else seemed to realize that – or care.

"You can fix a hen coop on your own, Jonas, really... if you've got time to fraternize with *Englischers*, you've got time to repair a hen coop," Aunt Alima said, tutting and shaking her head.

Jonas did not want to get angry in front of his *mamm*. It would only upset her, and he wanted her to get better as soon as possible. But as he went back downstairs, to face the dozens of tasks remaining that day, he could not help but feel as though something had to change if he was not to go quite mad, and the family break apart...

CHAPTER NINE

"Working in a flower store? Isn't there more to life than this?" Jack asked as Eve pointed to her place of work.

"It's Annie's store. I help her. I'm going to be in charge of it when she has her *boppli*," Eve replied feeling pride in her job despite his derision.

In Philadelphia, she had worked as a waitress in a restaurant, at the beck and call of customers day and night. The flower store was hardly a comedown. Eve loved working with Annie – making bouquets, cutting the flowers, and serving customers. She was happy, and it hurt her to think that Jack considered such a role beneath her. What did he expect? She was an ordinary woman with a *boppli* to support. She needed a job, and she would be forever grateful to Annie for giving her one.

"But is this it? Will you stay here for the rest of your life?" Jack persisted.

Eve had to admit she had not thought a great deal about her long-term prospects. But Faith's Creek was her home, and she felt ready to commit to the *Ordnung* and become a part of the community. She knew she had her detractors, and she was glad to see no sign of Alima Byler or her friends in the market square. But on the whole, the residents of Faith's Creek had welcomed her with open arms, and for the first time in her life, Eve felt a part of something bigger than herself.

"I don't know. Who knows the answer to such a question? For now, it's my home. They've been good to me, Jack," she replied.

Eve did not finish her sentence. She wanted to tell him that the people of Faith's Creek had been better to her than he had been, but to do so would be churlish, and now he was back, Eve could not help but feel some of those old feelings she had for him...

"It's not much of a life though, is it? Working in a flower store, the same old, same old, each day. You won't be happy," he persisted.

"And what right have you got to tell me what makes me happy?" she snapped.

He had gone too far, and Eve fixed him with a defiant look, as they stood at the door of the flower store. The last thing she wanted was to have him insult Annie.

"Look... I'm just saying, it's a very different life from what you're used to. I know they've been kind to you, but can it really be forever?" he asked.

Eve took a deep breath. She knew what he was doing. He would try to persuade her to return to Philadelphia with him. The thought had its attractions. She had been happy there – at least she had always believed she was happy. Growing up, Eve had heard only bad things about Faith's Creek, and her parents had led her to believe the life of the Amish was one of denial and restriction. They had told her nothing of the simple freedoms she now enjoyed – freedom from a world that was so busy and noisy, and where you never had time to stop and think about things that really mattered.

"I don't know, Jack. I'd like to say it could be. But... well, come and meet Esau. That's why you're here, isn't it?" Eve said, beckoning him to follow her.

His words were unsettling, and now she thought back to Philadelphia, and about the life she had known there. Annie was holding Esau, feeding him from a bottle, and she looked up in surprise as Eve and Jack entered the flower store.

"I thought you'd got lost," she said, raising her eyebrows.

"Oh... Annie, sorry, this is... Jack, Esau's *daed*," Eve said, as Jack stepped forward and held out his hand.

"A pleasure to meet you, Annie," he said.

Annie looked somewhat perturbed. Eve had explained the manner in which Jack had treated her – how he had gone off with another woman and left her alone with the *boppli*. In Annie's eyes, Jack was the one to blame for the events of the previous year, and she nodded to him, handing Esau to Eve and returning behind the counter.

"I'm sure," she replied.

"Jack's come to meet Esau," Eve said, turning to Jack, who looked down at the baby and smiled.

"I brought him something. It's not much, but I thought it would be a start," he said, and from his pocket he pulled out a small teddy bear with a smiling face, which he held out to Esau, who promptly began to cry.

"He's been crying ever since you left," Annie said, looking up from a bunch of flowers she was wrapping.

Eve tried to shush the *boppli*, looking embarrassed, as Jack continued to hold out the teddy bear in the awkward fashion of one who knows nothing about *kinner*.

"Oh... I'm sure he'll calm down. Let's sit down with him," Eve said, beckoning Jack to follow her into the storeroom behind the counter.

Annie gave her a look as she passed, and Eve knew her cousin-in-law did not approve. She sat down on an upturned packing crate in the storeroom, shushing Esau, as Jack sat down next to her.

"He's certainly got a fine pair of lungs on him," he said.

Eve smiled. "He's such a good *boppli* usually. But when he cries... he cries," she replied.

"Can I hold him?" Jack asked.

Eve felt a sudden reluctance at the thought of passing Esau to his *daed*. She knew it was wrong to think like that. But Jack's sudden appearance had upset the apple cart, and she was still uncertain as to his motives. *What should she do?*

CHAPTER TEN

But whatever her feelings toward him – and these were confused – he *was* Esau's *daed*, and the *boppli* she loved more than anything in the world was the result of their union. Eve could not deny that, and now she nodded, passing Esau gently into Jack's arms. He was still crying, and Jack looked thoroughly uncomfortable, despite the request being his own.

"There, now, just support his head, that's it, and don't hold him too tightly, that's right," Eve said, sitting back, though ready to spring forward should anything happen.

Jack cradled Esau in his arms, and still, he would not stop crying. His little face was screwed up tight and his cheeks were red. The sound was deafening and she could see that Jack was worried.

"What am I doing wrong?" he asked, looking up at Eve with an expression of disappointment on his face.

"You're not doing anything wrong. Babies cry. That's just natural," she replied, and he nodded, shushing Esau, who simply would not stop crying.

It was not long before Jack handed him back, and with much cradling, he eventually fell asleep.

"I should go, I suppose," Jack said, rising to his feet.

Eve felt sorry for him. If he had come to Faith's Creek in the expectation of stepping effortlessly into the role of Esau's *daed*, he would surely be disappointed. It was not that simple, she had found that out herself.

"Where are you staying? How long will you be here for?" Eve asked.

"I'm rented a room at the motel in Bird-in-Hand. I'll be here for the next few days. But Eve... I came here for a reason. Not just to see Esau, but to see you, too. I've missed you, Eve." He held her gaze, staring at her as if she were water in the desert. It was something he was good at and she must be careful not to fall for it again. "I was a fool to let you go," he said.

Eve's heart skipped a beat. Even though she knew him and his way of operating, she had not expected him to say such a thing. A *daed* wanting to bond with his son was one thing, but Jack had left her for another woman. He had wanted nothing to do with her – or Esau – and now he claimed to have missed her. Her life was different now – very different – and the thought of picking up where they had left off seemed an impossibility. But even though she didn't want to, Eve couldn't help but feel something of her past feelings for him, and as strange as it seemed, she found his words attractive.

"I... I've missed you, too. But... there's so much water under the bridge..." she began, just as Annie's voice came from the front of the store.

"It's time to close up now, Eve," she said.

Eve looked at Jack, who gazed back at her imploringly.

"I'll be in Bird-in-Hand. I'll come back to Faith's Creek before I leave. Think about what I said, Eve," he said, and nodding to her, he left the store, calling out a farewell to Annie, who did not respond.

Eve followed him out of the storeroom, and her cousin-in-law turned to her and raised her eyebrows.

"Well?" she asked.

Eve explained what had transpired in the diner and the storeroom, and Annie listened, shaking her head and tutting.

"He wants me to think about going back to Philadelphia," Eve said as her account came to an end.

Annie stared at her in disbelief.

"But you can't. You're settled here. You've been studying the *Ordnung*. You've said yourself what Faith's Creek means to you," she said, shaking her head.

"I know that... it's just... he's Esau's *daed*, and he wants to be a part of his life. I can't deny him that," she said.

Annie ushered her out of the flower store.

She knew how ungrateful she must sound. Annie, Marshall, and her Aunt Linda had done everything for her, and her words must have seemed like a slap in the face. Annie treated Esau as her own – he *had* been her own in the aftermath of Eve abandoning him amongst the flowers, and Eve knew how much the *boppli* would be missed, not only by Annie but by so many others in Faith's Creek, whose kindness Eve could never repay.

"He didn't have much trouble denying it when it suited him. And now he walks back into your life, expecting you to follow when he whistles," Annie replied, slamming the door with such force the windows rattled.

"I know. I know what he is like and I don't want to fall for it again, I haven't decided anything yet. He only put the thought in my mind just now. I haven't made a decision. I can't make a decision like that. Not alone," Eve said, knowing she had created a storm with her words.

What would her Aunt Linda say when she heard about it? And Marshall, too?

"If you go back to Philadelphia, you'll lose all the support you've got here. You'll be on your own, Eve. And what happens when he gets bored again?" Annie replied.

Eve had no answer for this. It was her fear, too, and as she followed Annie across the market square, she knew she must be certain before she did anything rash. But the arrival of Jack had made her question – quite unexpectedly – her feelings towards her new life. There those in Faith's Creek who would not be sorry to see the back of her, and with that in mind, she wondered if giving Esau a family, a *mamm,* and a *daed*, was what was right.

"I don't know... I don't know anything at the moment. But I can't just dismiss him out of hand. He's Esau's *daed*, and he wants to be a part of his life. I can't deny him that," Eve replied.

Annie turned to her and sighed. "I just want what's best for you and Esau," she replied.

Eve smiled. "I know you do. And I couldn't have asked for anyone kinder than you to be at my side through all of this. But perhaps it's time I stood on my own two feet for once," Eve replied.

There was no doubt that she was torn, and her now familiar life in Faith's Creek seemed suddenly unfamiliar. But Eve had not yet made up her mind, and despite the attractions of Jack's offer, she knew she had a lot to think about...

CHAPTER ELEVEN

"There you are, a dry roof over your heads. Now, I want to see some results from you. We need eggs, ladies," Jonas said, as he nailed the last of the felt roof tiles to the top of the hen coop.

He had worked alone. Levi had found another excuse not to help, and Jonas had got up extra early that morning to finish the milking, before repairing the roof of the hen coop. He had barely slept the night before, and it seemed as though one day blended into another, time passing by in a whirl. He had so many jobs to do and was torn in so many directions.

"I could've helped you with that," Henry said, coming around the corner of the barn.

"It's all right, you had the fence to mend, and I can't go up the ladder to fix the guttering. You know what I'm like with heights," Jonas said, as he stood back to survey his handiwork.

"It's all right. I'll go up the ladder. I don't mind doing that. But neither of us should be doing it. Levi has a pair of legs. Why doesn't he do it?" Henry said, shaking his head angrily.

"Because Levi gets away with everything, he..." Jonas began, but his words were interrupted by the person in question, as Levi shouted to them from the porch.

"Did I hear you talking about me?" he asked, striding towards them across the yard.

"I'm not ashamed to say you did, *jah*. We were talking about the fact that you don't pull your weight. In fact... you don't do anything," Henry said, as their brother swaggered up to them with a smirk on his face.

"You'd better talk to *Daed*, then. He'll tell you I don't have to do it. You can't force me. I'm the youngest, I don't have the same responsibilities as you," Levi replied, facing Jonas and Henry defiantly.

"But don't you want to work, Levi?" Jonas asked.

He could not understand his brother's attitude. It was as though Levi purposefully wanted to see the farm fail, and his family's livelihood destroyed.

"*Nee*, I don't. I don't want to milk cows and repair chicken coops. Why should I? I don't want to be a farmer. I want to do something else. I won't be stuck here in Faith's Creek for the rest of my life like the two of you," he exclaimed, turning away and marching off across the farmyard.

Jonas sighed. Despite his anger, he could sympathize with Levi's words. Ever since they had been *kinner*, the three brothers had been raised as farmers. That was their lot in life, or so their *daed* had taught them to believe, and whilst Jonas was happy with his life, he knew Levi was not.

"Leave him be," Jonas said, as Henry made a move to go after Levi, who was now disappearing down the track towards Faith's Creek.

"He just gets away with it. He does nothing but still expects to live under our roof, eat our food... it makes me so angry," Henry said.

"He's still young... I'm not defending him, but... maybe he *does* need to go off on a *rumspringa* and see what he thinks he's missing out on," Jonas replied.

"Why should he? We didn't get to go on a *rumspringa*. *Daed* told us we had to stay here and see to our responsibilities. But he never talks to Levi about responsibility, does he?" Henry said, sighing and shaking his head.

"I know it's not fair, but... well, let's get on with the next thing. You go up the ladder, and I'll bring the hay in for the cattle," Jonas said.

The two brothers worked hard that morning. There was, as ever, a lot to do, and after a simple noon meal of bread and cheese, they resumed their work. Jonas worked hard, but there was only so much he and Henry could do between them. Jobs inevitably went undone, and by mid-afternoon, Jonas had had enough.

"We've been up since four o'clock this morning. Let's call it a day," Henry said, straightening up and mopping his brow with a handkerchief.

"You're right. We've done enough for now. I could do with a walk," Jonas said.

He liked to walk, especially down by the creek. Walking helped him to think, and thanking his younger brother for his hard work, Jonas set off down the hill from the farm, taking a path across the cornfields and into the woods. It was a beautiful spring afternoon, the trees were blossoming and the birds singing. After the heat of working on the farm, Jonas was glad of the coolness of the water's edge, and took a familiar path upstream, pausing at a deep pool, where he threw stones into the water, watching as the ripples spread out.

"Is this really it?" he asked himself.

He was coming to resent his life. Perhaps Levi was right to rebel against expectations and desire a life different from the one they were living. It pained him to admit it, but Jonas did not want to be a farmer forever. He had ambitions, though he was unsure where they would take him.

But I can't leave Mamm, not now, and what about Henry? he thought to himself.

Like it or not, Jonas had responsibility, and he could not shirk it in the manner of his brother. He was lost in these thoughts when the sudden cry of a *boppli* caused him to startle. It was rare to meet anyone down by the creek, and looking up, Jonas was surprised to see the woman from the flower store, holding her *boppli* and looking at him in embarrassment.

"Oh, I'm sorry," she said, as Jonas turned.

"It's all right, I wasn't paying attention. You're Eve, aren't you?" he said.

She seemed surprised he knew her name, and he smiled at her as she stepped forward.

"That's right... did we...?" she asked.

"I came into the flower store the other day. I think you were distracted by the *boppli*," Jonas said, and now a look of recognition came over her face.

"Again, I'm sorry... I remember now, *jah*. You bought yellow roses for your *mamm*. Is she not well?" Eve asked, stepping forward, and shushing the crying *boppli* in her arms.

"She's got some kind of flu. Doctor Yoder says she'll get better, but it's taking a while. She has her *gut* days and bad – won't you sit down?" Jonas replied, indicating a rock opposite him by the water's edge.

"I'll pray for her. I hope she'll get better soon," Eve said.

Jonas was surprised to hear her mention prayer. She was an *Englischer*, though she was dressed in a simple cotton dress and wore a *kapp* on her head. Jonas was a man of faith. His parents had raised all three of the brother as believers, though Levi had rebelled against that, too. Jonas always said his prayers, and recently he had been praying especially for his *mamm* and her recovery.

"That's really kind of you, *denke*," Jonas said, as Eve sat down on the rock and gazed out across the pool.

"I love coming here. It's so peaceful down by the creek. I don't understand why more people don't come down here, though I suppose I wouldn't want them to if they did," she said, laughing as Jonas smiled at her.

"I come down here a lot, too. It's not been easy at home lately. I come here for the peace and solace," he said.

She looked at him sympathetically. "I'm sorry to hear that," she said.

Jonas was surprised at the ease with which he felt able to talk to her. She seemed to understand difficulties, and now he was curious to learn more about her. He had heard his Aunt Alima's version of the story a dozen times, but Jonas was certain there was more to Eve's past than was made obvious.

"My younger brother doesn't pull his weight, and my *daed* won't discipline him. We've got no help on the farm, and it's down to my brother, Henry, and I, to keep the place going. We've got a dairy herd, it's too much..."

he said, stopping, as he felt suddenly embarrassed at opening his thoughts to a near-stranger.

But Eve nodded and smiled, cradling the now sleeping *boppli* in her arms.

"I understand. Families can be difficult. It's a very different way of life here, isn't it?" she said.

Jonas had never known anything *but* this way of life, and now his curiosity about Eve's past was peaked.

"You came from Philadelphia, didn't you?" he asked.

Eve nodded. "That's right. I lived there all my life. But my parents came from Faith's Creek, originally. I grew up hearing what an awful place it was, but... it's proved to be my salvation," she replied.

"Are you planning to stay here and make a commitment to the community?" Jonas asked.

Eve smiled. "We'll see. I've been happy here. I can't deny that."

"It can't have been easy with the *boppli*," Jonas said. He could hear his aunt's words of condemnation, but Jonas could feel no animosity towards Eve. Quite the opposite, in fact. Everyone made mistakes, and he could only imagine how she must have felt to find herself pregnant and all alone in a big city. Was it any wonder she had returned to her roots? The likes of Aunt Alima would condemn her, but Jonas had always understood his faith as a faith of charity and forgiveness. Everyone deserved a second chance, and if Eve was to embrace the Amish way of life and take on the *Ordnung*, she surely deserved respect for doing so.

"It wasn't easy at all. I had to overcome a lot of difficulties. But with a *boppli*, you make sacrifices. You've got to," she said, glancing down at the sleeping boy and smiling.

"I admire you," Jonas said, and Eve looked up at him with an expression of gratitude on her face.

"That's very kind of you to say. I'm sorry... what's your name?" she asked.

Jonas blushed. He was not used to talking to women, not on such intimate terms at least. He felt a fool for forgetting to tell her his name.

"I'm Jonas, Jonas Byler. My family owns the dairy home or Caracass Hill, just a mile or so outside of the community," he said, pointing in the vague direction of the farm.

"I'm glad to meet you, Jonas. And this is Esau," Eve said, sitting the *boppli* up on her lap, his eyes still closed and fast asleep.

"He's perfect. I'm glad you've found the solace and peace you deserve," Jonas said.

"Not everyone thinks that. There are some..." Eve began, but Jonas interrupted her.

"I know, and for what it's worth, I don't share their opinions. My Aunt Alima's one of them, but she's horrible to everyone. She thinks because she goes to service every fortnight and reads her Bible every morning, that she's got a right to laud it over everyone else. But it's not true," he said, and Eve smiled.

"You're not responsible for your aunt's words. Don't worry. I won't hold them against you," she said.

Jonas blushed again, that was nice to know. "I just didn't want you to think... well, I wonder... do you know many people in Faith's Creek? It's just... well, there's a board game night every month in Taylor Peterson's barn. It's not much, I'm sure, after Philadelphia... but if you'd like to go, I'd be glad to go with you. It's happening tomorrow evening," Jonas said.

He did not know where the courage to ask such a forward question had come from, but to his surprise, Eve smiled and nodded.

"It's hard to meet anyone when you've got a *boppli*. I've made friends with some of the quilting circle. They're very nice, but they're all older than me. I'd be glad to come to the board games evening with you," she replied.

Jonas could not believe his luck, and as they continued to talk, he found himself ever more at ease with Eve, and wondering where this new friendship might lead...

CHAPTER TWELVE

Eve had not intended to bump into anyone that afternoon. She had gone for a walk by the creek with Esau to clear her head. Her thoughts were on Jack and his offer for her to return, with him, to Philadelphia. She felt torn between possibilities. There were those in Faith's Creek who would be glad to see her leave and others who would not. Meanwhile, her old life in Philadelphia beckoned. Eve was beginning to wonder if the best thing for Esau was to have a *mamm* and a *daed* to take care of him. But her thoughts had been interrupted as she had come across Jonas, and his kind words and the invitation to the board games evening. This had acted as a balm to soothe her soul. They had parted with the promise of seeing one another that coming Friday.

"He was nice, wasn't he, Esau?" Eve said as she walked up the path toward her aunt's house, carrying the *boppli* in her arms.

Annie was sitting on the porch with a ledger on her lap, writing in the day's profits, and she looked up from her figures and greeted Eve as she approached.

"Did the walk help to clear your head?" she asked.

Since Jack's arrival, Annie and Eve had been at loggerheads. Her aunt and cousin had sided with the flower store owner, and Eve had found herself outnumbered. They didn't want her to give any consideration to Jack's proposal of her leaving with him.

"I think I should give his proposal some thought," Eve had said.

Her aunt shook her head and had been firm with her. "There is no proposal. He's put an unwanted idea in your mind, and now you're doubting everything. He could up and leave again, just as he did last time. Why would you throw this life away for one so unworthy?"

Eve knew that was right, why would she? Now, she felt guilty for even mentioning it. Her aunt and cousin had done so much for her, and Annie had been stalwart in defending her. But Eve knew this was her choice to make, and hers alone. She could not simply agree to a life in Faith's Creek without considering the possibility of an alternative. Nothing was yet fixed, she had told Jack to wait for her decision. But time was passing, and whilst Jonas had been kind in his offer of accompanying her to the board games evening, Eve was beginning to think her future might lie elsewhere...

Annie cleared her throat and Eve was brought back to the present.

"I think so, I met someone down by the creek, a man. You might know him," Eve said.

Annie closed the ledger and looked up at her. "Don't forget, I'm still something of an outsider myself. What's his name?" Annie asked.

"Jonas... Jonas Byler. Is it like Bishop Beiler?" Annie asked, suddenly making the connection.

"I think it's spelled differently, and they're not related. His family owns the dairy farm on Caracass Hill, don't they? I think Marshall knows him. Did the two of you get on well?" Annie asked.

Eve blushed. She was not sure if this was a romantic liaison, even as she had felt glad to be introduced to Jonas and hear something of his story.

"He was nice, *jah*. I... he invited me to a board games evening in a barn at one of the farms. It sounds so old-fashioned, doesn't it? Back in Philadelphia, I'd go to the movies or the bowling alley or hang out at the mall with my friends, or... boys," she said, suddenly feeling embarrassed.

"And did it make you happy? All that consumer culture?" Annie asked.

Eve thought for a moment. The truth was, it did not make her happy. She remembered some words from a sermon given by Bishop Beiler some months previously. He had asked each member of the congregation to consider what they would like to be remembered about them when they died – would it be the things they had owned? The places they had been? The family they had raised? Or the person they had been?

"I've never given a eulogy listing the number of plows a farmer owned, or how many dresses a woman wore in her lifetime," he had said.

The things of the past had not made Eve happy. Quite the opposite, in fact. It was simple things that made her happy – hearing Esau gurgling in his crib or watching the sunlight on the waters in the creek.

"Not really. I suppose I thought it did at the time, but... *nee*, it didn't make me happy. I felt as if something was missing," Eve admitted.

"There's your answer, then," Annie replied.

"And you think I should pursue a friendship with him? I hardly know him. He came into the store to buy yellow roses for his *mamm*. That's all I know – and what he told me this afternoon," Eve said, feeling confused.

"Every person has a first meeting, however close they grow to the person in question. We all have to meet. Maybe this meeting was meant to be. Don't you trust in *Gott* to lead you in the right direction?" Annie asked.

Eve feared her cousin-in-law was suggesting *Gott* was steering her in the direction of remaining in Faith's Creek, but what if the opposite was true? She had prayed about her future, and the answer remained uncertain. Meeting Jonas had only added to her confusion.

"He was just being friendly, I'm sure," Eve said, though there was no denying she had felt something for the farmer's son, an affinity in circumstance which had led to an understanding between them.

"And aren't you glad about that? Isn't that what you want. You're learning the *Ordnung*, and you're about to take steps to join the community. Meeting a man like Jonas is a part of the journey. I don't know him well, but from what I've heard of him – and Marshall knows him through the store – he's a *gut* and upright man. A *Gott*-fearing man, and he's going to make someone a *gut* husband one day. Why can't it be you?" Annie asked.

Eve looked at her in surprise. It was one thing to want to return to her roots and rejoin the community her parents had rejected, but quite another to make plans to marry a man she barely knew. Eve knew things were different in Amish communities – the idea of dating was, compared to the wider world, outdated. There was an innocence to it, and whilst she had taken Jonas' invitation to the board games evening as a friendly gesture, she realized now there was more to it than just an evening in a draughty barn.

"I... I don't know. It's all too soon. He's nice, but I barely know him. I suppose I'll find out more about him, won't I," she said.

Annie nodded. "I know things are different here. But the outside world... well, it seems you've got a hard choice to make, give it time, Eve," she said.

Eve nodded. "I know that, Annie. But whatever choice I make, I want you to know how much you and Marshall and Aunt Linda mean to me. You were there for me when I needed it the most, and I won't forget that. Not ever," she said.

Annie smiled, and it seemed her mood had softened." "I just want the best for you, that's all," she replied.

That was what Eve wanted, too, except she was uncertain what the best really was, and whether she knew how to choose it.

CHAPTER THIRTEEN

"That's right, don't make the stitch too wide. I always make *boppli* clothes with the smallest of stitches. You can't trust a *boppli* not to pull things apart in a moment," Anna Troyer said, smiling at Eve, as she watched her make a third stitch in the cardigan she was sewing for Esau.

Eve enjoyed going to the quilting circle, even though she had found her skills less than a match for the older women. They could embroider a blanket in an afternoon, or make a jumper in the course of an evening, all while carrying on a conversation.

"I like the blue wool, he looks so sweet in blue," Eve said, glancing at Esau, who was sleeping in his basket at her feet.

He was almost too big for it, and it seemed he grew bigger every week, with clothes he had worn the previous month no longer fitting.

"It looked lovely, Eve. You've got a real talent," Sarah Beiler said, leaning over from her own work to look at that of Eve.

The women of the quilting circle had been unfailingly welcoming, and it was they who had encouraged Eve in her study of the *Ordnung*. All of them were committed to the faith and were shining examples of what was best about Faith's Creek and its community. Amongst them, Eve felt inadequate. There were other young *mamms* there too – Naomi, Sadie, Martha... they were all such *gut mamms*, dedicated to their *bopplis* and Eve often wondered what they must think of a woman who had abandoned her *boppli* as Eve had. But if they thought anything, they had never said it, and they had been nothing but kind to Eve as she settled into her new life amongst them.

"Oh, *denke*, that's kind, but it's nothing compared to the rest of you," Eve said, smiling at Sarah, who shook her head.

"A garment made by a *mamm* is more precious than anything anyone else could give. It's made with love, and that's all that matters – whether it takes you a day, a week, or a month," she replied.

Eve smiled. She wondered what the bishop's *fraa* would say if she knew Eve was thinking about returning to Philadelphia. Bishop Beiler had done so much to help instruct her in the *Ordnung*, and Sarah was to be her sponsor at the ceremony.

"Sarah... have you ever had doubts about your faith?" Eve asked as she prepared to make another stitch in the cardigan.

The bishop's *fraa* looked at her curiously. "Do you mean doubts about *Gott* or doubts about the life I lead here?" she asked.

Eve sighed. "I just mean... *nee*, not about *Gott*. I believe in *Gott*. I trust in *Gott*, and I know I always will. But this way of life... it's so different from what I've known in the past," she said.

Sarah reached out and placed her hand on Eve's, looking at her with a reassuring smile. "It's natural to doubt at times, and this way of life leads to questions, too. It's not the same as living in the outside world and going to church on a Sunday, then forgetting it all until the next weekend. Perhaps I'm not being fair, but our way of life is all or nothing. Either you're in or you're out. That's difficult for some people to understand, but for us, it makes perfect sense. You've got to follow where *Gott* leads you, Eve. *Nee* one's going to be angry if you decide it's not for you," she replied.

Eve was disappointed. A part of her had hoped that Sarah, as the bishop's *fraa,* would condemn any possibility of her falling away from the path she had chosen. But she should have known better. None of these women held to ideas of hellfire and damnation. They would not condemn Eve for her choice – whichever way it went. But now, Eve was even more confused than before, and when she left the quilting circle later that afternoon, the choice she had to make remained stark.

"Do we stay or go, Esau?" she asked, looking down at the *boppli* asleep in his basket, and wishing he really could tell her what was best for him, and for her...

CHAPTER FOURTEEN

"I think that's everything. He should be all right, I've put him down now, and he doesn't usually wake up, he's..." Eve said, but she was interrupted by her cousin-in-law, in an exasperated tone.

"Didn't I take care of him well enough before, Eve? I think I can manage, don't you? You'll only be gone for a few hours," Annie replied.

Eve blushed. "I'm sorry, I wasn't thinking. *Jah*, of course... I'm being foolish," she replied, checking her *kapp* and shawl in the mirror.

It was the evening of the gathering at Taylor Peterson's barn, and Eve was to meet Jonas at seven o'clock in the barn, where there would be board games set out and refreshments available. She had been looking forward to it all day and was grateful to Annie for minding Esau for the evening. But her cousin-in-law was right – Annie knew all too well how to take care of a *boppli*, and Eve felt bad for suggesting otherwise.

"Just go and enjoy yourself, Eve. You deserve it. You've had so much to think about recently. You need a break from it all," she said.

Eve nodded. She *was* feeling weary, and the opportunity to meet with Jonas and spend time getting to know him was something she was glad of, even as her heart remained torn between Faith's Creek and Philadelphia. She had not seen Jack again since the day of his arrival, but she knew he would be waiting for her decision, and the clock was ticking...

"You're right, I *have* been thinking a lot," she said, sighing, as she pulled her shawl more tightly around her shoulders.

"Don't think about it too much tonight. Enjoy the evening, I hope it'll convince you to stay in Faith's Creek," Annie said, looking pointedly at Eve, who sighed.

"We'll see. I'd better get going," she said and calling out a *gutbye* to her aunt and Marshall, who were in the kitchen, Eve left the house.

It was about a mile to Taylor Peterson's barn, and the evening was warm and balmy. Eve took her time, lingering to look out over the cornfields towards the setting sun.

You won't get a view like that in Philadelphia, she thought to herself as a buzzard seemed to sail across the field as it searched for its supper. At the hedgerow, it took up to the sky and circled above her, its plaintive cry echoing through the night.

There was so much about Faith's Creek she would miss if she was to leave, and so much about Philadelphia she already missed in staying. But the place was less important than the people, and the more she thought about it, the more she felt as though Esau deserved a *daed* to look up to as an example. Whether Jack could be that *daed* remained an open question, but he at least had the right to try, or so Eve believed.

He's changed. He's told me he's changed, Eve thought to herself, as she made her way up the track toward the barn.

Up ahead, she could see a group of young people milling about the farmyard, and amongst them, she recognized several of those who had spoken unkindly of her. But Eve was not perturbed, she was going to meet Jonas, and it did not matter who else was there, too. She could see him standing by the barn door, waiting for her, and now she waved, hurrying towards him, as he smiled at her.

"I was just about to start walking down the track to meet you. I should've offered to walk you up here. But I've only just finished my job on the farm. My brother and I were clearing out gutters. Well, he went up the ladder, I'm terrified of heights," Jonas said, laughing and shaking his head.

Eve admired him for the determined way he went about his work. He had so much responsibility, and it made her think of the many ways in which she had shirked her own responsibilities in the past.

"It's all right, I found my way here. It's such a beautiful evening, isn't it?" she said, looking out over the corn-fields, with their gently swaying crop.

"It is, isn't it? Really beautiful. I'm glad you came. Shall we go inside?" he asked, offering Eve his arm.

She took it, smiling to herself at the formality of what they were doing. There were so many unwritten rules in a community such as this, and Eve knew Jonas would see this moment as the beginning of something between them. He was kind and sweet, a man for whom she could only have respect, and now she hoped he would not think she was leading him along, even as she knew her family wanted a match between them.

"I haven't played board games since I was a *kinner*," she said, glancing around the barn, where upturned hay bales were being used as tables, and groups of young people sat playing draughts and chess.

"It's fun. It brings people together. Shall we get some lemonade?" Jonas asked, pointing to a table of refreshments, with jugs of lemonade and plates of cinnamon cookies.

Eve nodded. She thought back to her "dates" in Philadelphia, meeting men in diners or fast-food joints or going to the movies. This was very different, but it felt right. In this new way of life, Eve was glad to have met Jonas and to share this time with him, even as she wondered where it might lead. They poured themselves each a glass of lemonade, but as they turned to find a group to join, Eve noticed several of the young women looking at her and whispering amongst themselves.

"I'm surprised you've got the nerve," one of them said.

Eve recognized her as Lydia Backwater, whose barbed comments she had encountered before.

"I'm sorry?" Eve said as Lydia stepped forward.

"Coming here after what you've done. Does Jonas know you were cozying up to the *boppli's daed* in the diner the other day?" she asked, fixing Eve with a stern gaze.

"I..." Eve began, faltering, for she had not realized anyone knew about Jack.

"You didn't think anyone overheard you, did you?" Lydia continued.

"Now, just a moment..." Jonas began, but he was interrupted by another of the women, who pointed her finger accusingly at Eve and tutted.

"You were talking about going back to Philadelphia. That's why he's come, isn't it? To take you and the *boppli* away. And yet here you are, leading Jonas along, making him think he's got a chance when you're about to run off back to the big city with your out-of-wedlock *boppli*, and the man you couldn't forget. You just used this community to get back on your feet, and now you'll run away. Admit it, Eve – that's what you're going to do, isn't it?" she said.

Tears welled up in Eve's eyes. Jonas would think she was nothing but a wicked creature, a disgrace to the faith she purported to uphold.

"It's not like that," she stammered, but she knew there could be no persuading her detractors that she was a *gut* person. In their eyes, Eve was guilty. They had judged her and found her wanting. She turned to Jonas, who looked confused.

"It seemed pretty clear in the diner. He's waiting for you in Bird-in-Hand. When were you going to tell Jonas?" Lydia asked.

Eve turned to Jonas, an imploring look on her face. "It's not like that, I promise you," she said, but Eve could see the seeds of doubt had already been planted.

"Then you deny it? That man wasn't the *boppli's daed* and you're not thinking about going back to Philadelphia?" Lydia said.

Eve could not deny it, and faced with such humiliation, she turned and fled, running from the barn, even as Jonas called out after her.

"Eve, wait..." he said, but Eve was gone, hurrying across the farmyard and down the track back towards her aunt's house.

Her mind was made up. She was not wanted in Faith's Creek, and now she knew there was only one option left... it was time to leave.

CHAPTER FIFTEEN

Jonas was angry. He turned to Lydia, looking at her incredulously. "Why did you do that? What's the meaning of it?" he exclaimed.

Lydia returned his stare defiantly. "She'd only have hurt you, Jonas. She was overheard in the diner talking to the *boppli's daed*. They were making plans to go back to Philadelphia. She's not welcome here," Lydia said, and the other women nodded.

"In your opinion? And who are you to say who's welcome and who's not?" Jonas said.

He was upset, even as he felt confused as to the confrontation. Eve was learning the *Ordnung*. She had spoken of her desire to remain a part of the community, and her affection for Faith's Creek and its ways. To hear Lydia's words brought all that into question, and Jonas found himself doubting his own words.

"I'm only telling you the facts, Jonas. She's not going to stay here. All her piety and *kapp* wearing. It takes more than that to live our way of life. She was never going to stay. She'll go back to Philadelphia and leave you with a broken heart. We're saving you from that," Lydia replied.

But Jonas was tired of other people telling him what to do. It was his life, and if he wanted to make a mistake of the heart, then so be it. But in Jonas's eyes, Eve was not a mistake – far from it. She was a woman with a past, but what person did not have a past? He thought back to his Aunt Alima's words. Lydia was no different. These people had made up their minds about Eve, and there was nothing she could say or do to defend herself.

"You don't know her. You don't know what she was going to do," he exclaimed.

"And you don't know her either. That's the problem with outsiders. They come here thinking they can just take up our way of life and be done with it. It takes more than a *kapp* and a pious look on your face. She's not committed, and she wouldn't be committed to you, either," Lydia replied.

Jonas shook his head. But doubts were already forming. He wanted to defend Eve, but Lydia was right – he did not know Eve, and as for these new revelations about her and Esau's *daed*...

"I... I don't know, but I don't judge people," he stammered.

Lydia shook her head. "Sometimes you need to," she replied.

Jonas did not feel like playing board games that evening. He returned home, brooding and ponderous. His *daed* was sitting on the porch, and as Jonas approached, he looked up at him in surprise.

"I thought you were out for the evening," he said.

Jonas shook his head. "It didn't work out. Like everything in my life," he replied.

His *daed* furrowed his brow. He was looking old and worn out, and now he rose to his feet and sighed. "You've not been yourself lately, Jonas," he said.

"I've not had a moment to be anything, *Daed*. I can't go on like this. I can't run this farm without help. You don't seem to understand that," he exclaimed.

Jonas's anger was boiling over. He knew it was wrong to shout at his *daed*, but he had reached the end of his tether.

His *daed* looked at him in surprise. "Jonas?" he said.

"I mean it, *Daed*. Something's got to change. I can't do this anymore," he replied, and he stormed up the porch steps and into the house, slamming the door behind him.

Levi was sitting on the couch, sprawled with his legs up reading a book. He looked up inquisitively at Jonas, a smirk coming over his face.

"Did you get bored of playing board games?" he asked.

"*Nee*, Levi. But I've got bored of this," Jonas exclaimed, and before his brother could reply, he had marched upstairs, shutting himself in his bedroom and throwing himself onto the bed.

"*What a mess,*" he thought to himself, but despite what he had heard about Eve that evening, Jonas could not help but think of her, and the more he thought of her, the more he knew there was certain to be another side of the story...

CHAPTER SIXTEEN

Eve's mind was in turmoil as she ran home that evening. She could hear the jeers and taunts of Lydia and Alima ringing in her ears. She was not wanted in Faith's Creek, and she had been a fool to think of herself as being so. The humiliation stung, and the look on Jonas' face had said it all. She could not stay amongst the community of believers a moment longer, and now she knew she had no choice but to accept Jack's offer and return to Philadelphia with Esau. As she entered the house, Annie looked up at her in surprise.

"You're back early, I was just going to check on Esau," she said.

Eve shook her head. "You don't need to. I'll check on him," she said, fighting back the tears.

Her aunt appeared from the kitchen, also looking surprised at the sight of Eve, who was not due back for several hours. "Has something happened, Eve?" she asked.

"It's... at the barn... the other women... they said such horrible things," she exclaimed, as she could not hold back her tears a moment longer.

Annie came hurrying over to her, putting her arms around her, and shushing her. "Oh, don't listen to them, Eve. They're just small-minded. It's only a few bad apples," she said.

Eve shook her head. "*Nee*... it's not... they told Jonas about Jack. They said I was planning to leave Faith's Creek, and I was just leading him on. You should've seen the look on his face. He believed them, I know he did," Eve sobbed.

Her aunt and cousin-in-law exchanged glances.

"But it's not true. You only spoke to Jack. He's Esau's *daed*. He wants to be involved, it's understandable, but... you're not seriously thinking about..." her aunt began.

Eve interrupted her. "I'm going to do it, Aunt Linda. I'm going back to Philadelphia. I shouldn't ever have come here. I'm sorry. I've been such a burden to you, and you've been so kind, but... I can't stay here. Not anymore, not the way I was treated, I'm not wanted," Eve replied.

"You're not thinking properly, Eve. You can't go back to Philadelphia," her aunt exclaimed.

But Eve's mind was made up. She would never be truly a part of the community in Faith's Creek. Lydia Bywater was right. A *kapp* and a few pious words did not make a person Amish. Her parents had rejected their faith, and Eve had grown up in a very different world. *That* was the world she belonged in, and there was no point in pretending differently. Jack would return from Bird-in-Hand the following day, and she would give him her decision then.

"But I've got to. It isn't right to keep Esau from his *daed*, and I don't belong here, not really. It was a mistake to come here, and it's a mistake to stay here," Eve replied.

She felt a fool, and whilst she knew just how much her family had done for her, Eve was certain she was now doing the right thing. She had fooled no one with her pious platitudes, and she had hurt a *gut* man in the process. Jonas was the innocent party. He had been kind to her, and she had led him on.

"But we want you here, Eve. We love having you here," her aunt said, taking Eve by the arm.

At that moment, Marshall appeared from outside. He had been tending to the vegetable garden, and he, too, looked confused at the sight of Eve, returned so early from the board games evening, with tears in her eyes.

"Is something going on?" he asked.

"Talk some sense into Eve, Marshall. She's talking about going back to Philadelphia. I wish that man hadn't put such thoughts into her mind," Linda said.

Marshall let out a cry of exclamation. "You... but you can't go back to Philadelphia, Eve. You're a part of this community now," he exclaimed.

"I've made up my mind, Marshall. I can't stay here any longer. It's not right. I'm sorry. You've all been so kind. But I've got to think about what's best for Esau," Eve said, shaking her head.

"And don't you think what's best for him is having a family who loves and cares for him?" Annie asked.

Eve knew she would be hurting her cousin-in-law by leaving. Annie had loved Esau as her own, and she doted on him. But her mind was made up, and it would not be changed.

"I'm going to bed. I'm sorry," she said, and turning, she hurried up the stairs, as tears rolled down her cheeks.

"Eve, pray about this," Linda called after her, but Eve was gone.

Upstairs, Esau was asleep in his cot, and she looked down at him and smiled, placing her hand gently on his chest.

"We'll be all right, won't we?" she whispered, even as her mind was filled with doubts and uncertainties.

She would pray, she had a big decision to make and she had to make the right one for Esau. What happened to her didn't matter. She did not think that she could love Jack again, at least not for a while, but the chance to give her *boppli* a proper family was too much to pass up.

CHAPTER SEVENTEEN

The next morning, Eve had still not changed her mind about leaving. She had prayed and cried and tossed and turned in the bed. Still, she believed it was the right thing to do, and she had already packed her things by the time Jack was due to arrive. She had arranged to meet him in the market square, outside the diner, and taking Esau, she left the house without saying goodbye, planning to return only to collect her things before boarding the Greyhound bus to Philadelphia. Eve did not want a long, drawn-out farewell. She knew her family would only try to change her mind about leaving, and whilst she felt guilty about having made such a decision, she felt certain it was for the best.

Pray about this, she thought to herself, echoing her aunt's words of the previous night.

But even though she had tried, Eve was finding it hard to pray. She was scared of the answer she would receive – would *Gott* punish her for making such a big decision and leaving Faith's Creek? But Eve already felt punished by those who ridiculed her and criticized her.

"I can't go on like this," she told herself, as she hurried towards the market square.

Eve's heart was beating fast. She could see Jack standing in front of the diner. What was he thinking? Esau began to cry, and she shushed him, bouncing him in her arms.

"Eve... I wasn't sure if you'd come," Jack said, as she came to meet him.

"I've made my decision. I'm coming back to Philadelphia," she said.

He looked at her in surprise, as though he had not been expecting her to say as much, even as a look of relief came over his face.

"Do you mean that? That's wonderful," he said.

Despite feeling cold and alone, she nodded. "I mean it. You're right. I don't belong here. I was a fool to think I did. I came back because I was desperate. But... it's not right," she replied, glancing across at the flower store, and recalling the happy times she and Annie had shared there.

"I thought you'd want to stay. You seemed so certain about it – about taking up the faith again," Jack said, as Eve cradled Esau in her arms.

"I was wrong about it... they don't want me here," she said, even though she knew she was telling only half a truth.

Sarah Beiler, Anna Troyer, the other women in the quilting circle... they would all be sad to see her go. And then there were the many customers she had served, so many of whom had told her how welcome she was in Faith's Creek. She thought of Bishop Beiler and his gentle words of encouragement as she explored the faith and asked questions about the Amish way of life.

"You've got lots of people praying for you," he had told her.

And now she thought of Jonas and his kind words by the creek. He had wanted to spend time with her and made an effort to welcome her. Was all that for nothing?

"Well... I'm glad you've changed your mind. It's a strange place. I can't wait to get back to Philadelphia," Jack said.

"I just need to collect my things from my aunt's house, then we can go," Eve said.

She knew she had to leave, and quickly. To stay would only lead to persuasion, and Eve was not about to risk another encounter with Alima Byler or Lydia Backwater. She couldn't bear the humiliation. Her decision was made, and there could be no going back.

"All right, I'm ready. Shall I take Esau?" Jack asked.

"He's your son," Eve said, forcing a smile to her face as she handed the *boppli* to his *daed*.

Eve did not know if she could love Jack as she once had. Perhaps too much water had passed under the bridge for that. But she was determined to try – if not for her own sake, then for Esau's. He deserved to see his parents together, and to grow up in a loving family – was that not what those like Alima and Lydia preached? Eve was not ashamed of her son, nor of her circumstances, and though it was with a heavy heart, she was leaving Faith's Creek, she was now certain she was doing the right thing.

"And you're certain you want this? You're still wearing that funny hat," Jack said.

Eve reached up and took off her *kapp*. It seemed a strange thing to cling to, even as she felt odd without it. She had become used to Faith's Creek, and the life she was living there, and taking off the *kapp* was like taking off the identity she had forged.

"I'll change once we're back in Philadelphia. I've still got some of my old clothes in the bag at my aunt's house," Eve replied.

They made their way across the market square, and Eve looked back at the flower store, taking a deep breath as she turned away, following Jack, who was carrying Esau in his arms, a backpack slung over his shoulders. The *boppli* was quiet now, and he stayed asleep until they reached Eve's aunt's house, where they found Annie and Marshall standing on the porch.

"We thought you'd gone without saying goodbye," Annie said, hurrying towards Eve.

There were tears in her eyes, and she threw her arms around Eve, the two women embracing, as Eve fought back the tears.

"I wouldn't do that... I'm here now, but we're leaving. We'll catch the next Greyhound bus. There's one due soon," Eve said, for she still had the timetable from the day of her arrival, never having entirely accepted her situation as it was.

Annie shook her head. "I wish you'd reconsider," she said, as Linda stepped out onto the porch.

"I've made you some sandwiches, and I've put some slices of cake in there, too," she said, handing over a tuck box.

"That's so kind of you, Aunt Linda," Eve said, and a tear rolled down her aunt's cheek.

"Write to me as soon as you're settled. I wish you'd reconsider. Why should a few bad apples spoil the batch?" she asked.

Eve shook her head. "Because it wasn't meant to be," she replied, and kissing her aunt goodbye, she bid her family farewell.

"I'll miss you, Eve – but promise me you'll come and visit, when the *boppli's* here, I mean. I don't know what I'll do in the flower store without you," Annie said, and as she kissed Eve goodbye, she pressed a book into her hand.

Eve looked down at it. It was Annie's Bible – thumbed from a lifetime, with all the marks of a dearly-loved book.

"I can't take this," she exclaimed, but Annie shook her head.

"I want you to have it. I want you to keep on studying the scriptures and never stop praying and asking for *Gott's* guidance. You've taken off your *kapp*, but don't lose your faith, Eve," she said.

Eve took the Bible. She knew it was Annie's most precious possession, her source of hope and guidance, and now she looked at her cousin-in-law with tears in her eyes.

"I... I don't know what to say, Annie," she said, but Annie pressed the Bible into Eve's hands, wanting her to take it.

"Just promise me you'll keep reading and knowing *Gott's* word," she whispered.

Eve nodded. Despite what everyone must think, she was not abandoning her faith. Eve still believed in *Gott's* guidance, even as that guidance seemed to be leading her away from everything she was familiar with.

"I promise," she replied, glancing back at Jack, who was looking impatient.

With their final farewells said, and Eve's aunt reminding her to write to them, Eve and Jack left for Philadelphia, catching the Greyhound bus, which trundled its way across the prairie and along the interstate back toward the big city. As she looked back across the cornfields in the direction of Faith's Creek, Eve felt as though she was waking from a dream – had it all been real?

"I'm making the right decision," she told herself. As she clasped Esau in her arms, and faced forward, Eve felt determined to make her old life work once again.

CHAPTER EIGHTEEN

Jonas was feeling miserable. He was worried about what Eve would think of him. He had done nothing to stand up for her, and she had fled before he had had time to apologize to her for the way she had been treated. He believed she must think he was like the others – like Lydia Backwater and Aunt Alima – judgmental and not approving of a woman who had given birth out of wedlock. But none of that mattered to Jonas. What mattered was a new start. Bishop Beiler would have called it repentance, and repentance meant new life and conversion. Eve wanted to be a part of the community of Faith's Creek, and it pained Jonas to think of the way that same community had rejected her. He did not want to be tarred with the same brush, or for Eve to think he had judged her.

She must hate me, he thought to himself.

It was early morning, and Jonas was alone in the milking parlor. He had asked Levi to help him, but his brother had remained in bed, and Henry was exhausted from doing the work of half a dozen men on the farm the previous day. Jonas hoped their *daed* would act – things could not go on as they were. His *mamm* was still bedridden, and Doctor Yoder had suggested it could be weeks before she made a full recovery.

And meanwhile, we go from bad to worse, Jonas thought to himself.

As dawn broke, Jonas finished the milking, returning to the house to find Henry making a pot of coffee in the kitchen.

"I thought you might like something to wake you. Thanks for covering for me this morning. I slept like a log," Henry said, as he placed the coffee pot on the table.

"It's all right. You covered for me last night. For all the *gut* it did," Jonas replied.

His brother looked at him curiously. Like Jonas, Henry rarely had time for pursuing romance. He had never entertained any serious courtship, and the two brothers had often despaired of ever settling down.

"I heard you come in and shout at Levi," Henry said.

Jonas rolled his eyes. "That's nothing new... but it didn't go well at the board games evening," he said, and then he explained what had transpired and how Lydia Backwater had stuck the knife in.

"How do you feel about it? The *boppli,* I mean? It's a big responsibility to take on," Henry said after Jonas had finished his explanation.

But the thought of taking on another man's *kinner* held no fear for Jonas. The more he thought about Eve, the more he wanted to be with her, and now he wondered if the possibility of an apology might still exist.

"I know she loves the *boppli,* and *kinner* come first. But... I just want a chance for something new. She's a breath of fresh air. I like her, I like her a lot," Jonas said, even as he knew he should have done more to stand up to Eve's detractors.

"Then go and tell her. Apologize for Lydia and Aunt Alima. They can think what they like. I don't know about you, but I'm tired of other people's opinions. Most people aren't like that. But when a vocal minority shouts, people listen – that's the sad fact in it all. But I gave up listening to Aunt Alima long ago, and so should you. If you like Eve, and you're willing to take on another man's *boppli,* then talk to her," Henry said.

Jonas smiled. His brother was more forthright than him, but Henry was right – he needed to speak to Eve, and having drunk a cup of coffee, he set out to walk to the flower store, hoping to speak to her.

* * *

The market square was busy that morning, the stalls set up in a semi-circle, selling all manner of goods. But Jonas was only interested in the flower store and feeling nervous, he paused outside, peering cautiously through the window for a glimpse of Eve.

"They're open, you know," a voice behind him said, and Jonas turned to find one of the stallholders – Monica Hertz, whose stall was outside the flower store and sold wool – smiling at him.

"Oh... *jah,* I... wasn't sure if they would be," Jonas replied.

Monica continued to smile at him. "Were you looking for Annie, or... Eve?" she asked.

Jonas blushed. He was not very *gut* at this, and he felt certain he was about to make a fool of himself. It had taken a considerable amount of courage on his part to invite Eve to the board games evening, and now he was unsure what he would say when he came face to face with her. But in his heart, Jonas knew he had to try. He had spent too long neglecting his own happiness for the sake of others, and he was not about to allow the possibility of something more with Eve to slip through his fingers. At the very least, Jonas wanted Eve to understand he was not like the others, nor did he share their opinion of her. He was falling in love with her, and her past did not matter.

"Eve," Jonas said.

"I didn't see her this morning, but you could ask Annie. Don't hold back, Jonas," Monica said, raising her eyebrows at Jonas, who blushed an even deeper shade of red.

It was as though Monica knew the feelings he had for Eve, and now he took a deep breath and nodded – this was the prompting he needed, a sign from *Gott* of what was meant to be.

"*Denke*," he replied.

The scent of the flowers was intoxicating, and Jonas breathed in the sweet scent, expecting to hear the cry of a *boppli* as he entered the flower store a moment later. The bell jangled above the door, and Annie appeared from the storeroom. She looked sad but forced a smile to her face at the sight of Jonas, who took off his hat and nodded to her.

"I... I was looking for Eve," Jonas said.

Annie shook her head. "Oh... I'm sorry, Jonas. It didn't work out for Eve. She's gone back to Philadelphia. She left on the Greyhound with Esau, and... Jack, Esau's *daed*," Annie replied.

Jonas' heart sank. He immediately blamed himself. Eve had surely left because she felt unwelcome in Faith's Creek. If only he had stood up to his aunt and Lydia. He furrowed his brow, looking at Annie and shaking his head.

"Oh, I didn't realize. It's just... well, the board games evening didn't exactly go to plan. Some women were there, you know the sort. They were saying things," Jonas mumbled, fearing Annie would blame him for Eve's return to Philadelphia.

He knew what Annie had done for the *boppli*, and he could only imagine how she must feel at having lost him, and Eve, to the bright lights of Philadelphia. But the flower store owner shook her head and sighed.

"She wasn't happy here, Jonas. Well, perhaps that's not true. I think she wanted to be. But she still had a past, and when that past came knocking, she opened the door. I know you liked her. She liked you, too. You were kind to her when she needed it. I'll not forget that," Annie replied.

"But did she really love him? Didn't he hurt her terribly?" Jonas asked.

He felt confused, wondering what it was this man had that he did not. Jack had treated Eve terribly, and now he had simply clicked his fingers and she had come running.

Annie shook her head. "I'd say he did, but love isn't always rational, I suppose," Annie replied.

Jonas did not know how to feel – should he think of himself as betrayed by Eve, or should he feel sorry for her. She had accepted his invitation to the board games evening and seemed happy in his company. But all the while, her heart had been elsewhere, and if not her heart, then her thoughts. She had still held a flame for Jack, and that fact made Jonas feel terribly sad.

"I understand. But is she happy?" Jonas asked.

Eve had seemed settled in Faith's Creek. She had been happy there. She had spoken of learning the *Ordnung* and being received into the faith. She had blossomed, like the flowers in the flower store, and returning to Philadelphia was surely a wilting of possibility.

"I don't know. I hope so. It's what I pray for. But I don't think she had a choice – not in her heart, at least. She must have felt torn between giving Esau a *daed* and finding happiness here in a community of faith. She was welcomed here. Only a few voices detracted from that welcome, but sometimes they are the loudest. The ones we here most. I tried to persuade her to stay, but her mind was made up. She's gone, and I don't know when we'll see her again," Annie replied.

Jonas felt sorry for her – and for himself. Once again, he had failed to grasp the possibility of happiness. He was left behind, and it was a terrible feeling. A sudden thought occurred to him, even as he tried to dismiss it as nonsense.

"She went back to Philadelphia. Do you know where she might be? An address, I mean," Jonas asked.

He knew it was foolish – absurd, in fact. But the thought of going to Philadelphia had now occurred to him. He knew he could not live with himself if he did not apologize to Eve for what had happened between them. Even though he knew rejection was a very real possibility, Jonas was determined to try. He had spent so long doing what others told him or expected of him. But this was something else – this mattered, and Jonas was not about to allow Eve to slip away without knowing how sorry he was for what had happened.

"Are you thinking of going after her?" Annie asked.

Jonas was embarrassed. It was foolish, he knew that, but a part of him did not care. He nodded, his decision made. "I need to tell her I'm sorry," he said.

Annie looked at him in confusion. "Sorry for what?" she asked.

"For not standing up for her. I let her go, and that's why she's gone, isn't it? She thinks I'm just like the others – Lydia Backwater and my Aunt Alima. But I'm not, and this community isn't like that. Perhaps if she knows that, she'll come back," Jonas replied.

He knew it was madness, but as Annie had said – love was not always rational. Jonas was determined to do what he could, and now he could think of nothing but finding Eve and telling her just how sorry he was. Would it bring her back? Jonas did not know, but he felt only the prompting of something beyond himself to try.

"I hope she does. I don't know if she will, but if you're willing to try, I won't try to stop you," Annie said.

She took out a piece of paper and scribbled down an address, handing it to Jonas, who looked down at it and nodded. He had never been to Philadelphia. He knew nothing of city life, or what to expect. The words meant nothing to him, but he would find the address, and in finding Eve, perhaps...

"I'm going to try," Jonas replied, and taking a deep breath, he pocketed the piece of paper, and bidding Annie goodbye, stepped out onto the market square, feeling suddenly filled with possibility, even as he feared that possibility could be rejection, too.

CHAPTER NINETEEN

"Y ou're going where?" Jonas's *daed* asked.

Jonas pushed clothes into a bag, glancing around him and wondering what he might have forgotten. "I'm going to Philadelphia, *Daed*. I won't be too long."

His *daed* looked at him in astonishment – he could not have been more surprised if Jonas had announced he was going to the moon. "But you can't go. You're needed here. The farm."

Jonas put down the bag and straightened up. He turned to his *daed*, summoning all his courage as he fixed him with an angry gaze. "Levi can do it, *Daed*, or you can employ someone to help. I've done my share. I'll only be away for a few days. But I'm going, and there's nothing you can do to stop me." He knew he shouldn't be angry, that he had let this situation build for too long, but he was. Maybe, this was what was needed for the family to see that things needed to change.

His *daed* stepped back in surprise. Jonas never answered back. He always did as he was told, but not this time.

"But why? Why Philadelphia?"

Jonas returned to his packing. "I'm going to find Eve – the woman I took to the board games evening," he said.

Jonas knew how it sounded – it was an astonishing thing to do. He hardly knew Eve, and now he was going to travel to Philadelphia in search of her. He had never traveled so far, and he did not know what to expect when he arrived there. But Jonas knew he was being led – he trusted *Gott's* prompting. It was important to him that Eve understood that he did not share the views of those others who had driven her away. She may have made up her mind about Jack, but he wanted to change her mind about Faith's Creek and hopefully, about him. Why did it matter so much, why did he feel so drawn to her? He didn't know but he knew he would regret it for the rest of his life if he did not try.

"And the milking? Who's going to see to that?" his *daed* asked.

"Levi knows how to milk a cow, *Daed*. He might not do it very often, but he knows," Jonas replied, and before his *daed* could respond, Jonas had called out a goodbye to his *mamm* and left the house.

"How did he take it?" Henry asked, for Jonas had already explained the situation to his brother beforehand.

"Just as I expected. I told him Levi could take the strain. But you need to tell him, too. I'm sorry I'm going away, I'll be back soon, and..." Jonas began, but his brother interrupted him.

"You don't need to apologize, Jonas. You work harder than anyone. I'll milk the cows, and if the rest of the jobs don't get done, so be it. But I'm tired of it, too. *Daed* needs to make Levi do some work, and if he won't do that, he'll soon see what happens when one of us isn't here to pick up the pieces. Go to Philadelphia. I can see what it means to you." Henry said, and the two brothers embraced, nodding to one another, as they parted.

Jonas made his way out of the farmyard.

It felt odd to be leaving Faith's Creek. Bird-in-Hand was as far as Jonas had ever gone, apart from a brief visit to relatives in the north of the state. Faith's Creek was all he knew, and now he was setting off for Philadelphia with only a scribbled address and hope in his heart.

He walked to the Greyhound stop, every step made him feel more confident. Even if she turned him away, he had tried and that was what life was about. Doing your best and sticking to your principles. He arrived at the bus stop and checked the timetable. He was lucky, a bus would arrive in the next half hour. It would take most of the day to get to Philadelphia, and as he waited, Jonas felt like changing his mind. One moment, he was confident, the next, filled with guilt for abandoning the farm. The bus pulled up and the door whooshed open.

"Are you getting on son?" the driver asked when Jonas was rooted to the spot.

He nodded and climbed aboard asking for a ticket to Philadelphia.

"Do you want a return?" the driver asked, as Jonas nervously bought his ticket.

"Oh... yes, I want to come back," Jonas said, handing over the payment.

The bus was only carrying a few passengers, and Jonas settled down at the back, looking out of the window, as the bus sped off along the road which would eventually join the interstate. As the cornfields disappeared, and they drove through woodland, passing the occasional farmstead, Jonas could only imagine what he would find on reaching Philadelphia.

I just hope I'm doing the right thing, he thought to himself, even as he knew he had to try. Everything was so different and he felt a touch of fear. He wanted to scream, stop, and run home, but he wouldn't. Closing his eyes he began to pray and his nerves left him

* * *

"Filbert Street bus station, end of the line," the driver called out.

Jonas was startled, opening his eyes and sitting up. He had fallen asleep somewhere on the interstate, and now he awoke to find his fellow passengers disembarking. Looking out of the window, he could see a bleak sight – the bus station, with its grey concrete structure looming over the buses, parked side by side in their bays. Crowds were milling, and there was noise coming from every direction.

"Excuse me, do you know where Pine Street is?" Jonas asked as the driver climbed out to light a cigarette on the sidewalk.

"What am I, a street map? You're near Chinatown and Center City here, after that, find your own way," the driver said, shaking his head.

The address Annie had given was 142 Pine Street – an apartment building, or so she had thought. But after that, she had known nothing about its whereabouts. Everywhere seemed so big, and as Jonas left the bus station, he looked around him in confusion as to which way to go.

"Dollar for directions?" a man said, stumbling towards Jonas, who backed away in surprise.

The man had a wild look in his eyes, which were bloodshot, and his clothes were scruffy and unkempt. He was holding a map, pointing at the road layout.

"I... no, it's all right, thank you," Jonas said, turning and hurrying off down the nearest street.

It was a little quieter here, and he paused outside a café, where a flashing neon sign announced, *"coffee and donuts."*

It was around five o'clock, and Jonas was grateful for having arrived in Philadelphia in daylight, even as he was finding it difficult to get his bearings. He stepped into the café, where a tall man in an apron and open white shirt, standing behind the counter, greeted him warmly.

"Take a seat, I'll be right over – come in from the country, have you?" he asked, smiling.

Jonas sat down at the nearest table with relief. "I've come from Faith's Creek," he said, and the man nodded.

"Amish country, isn't it?" he asked.

"That's right. I've come to find... a friend," Jonas said, for it did not seem right to explain his business to a complete stranger.

"Coffee?" the man asked, holding up a pot, and Jonas nodded.

The café was pleasant, decorated with old black and white photos of Philadelphia, and on the counter was a large selection of cakes, including a red velvet cake, which looked delicious.

"You don't happen to know where Pine Street is, do you?" Jonas asked.

"I can look on a map. We get lots of visitors in here. You can take one," the man said, and having poured Jonas a cup of coffee, he produced a tourist map of the city, on which the two of them were able to locate Pine Street, some eight blocks down from City Hall.

"Thank you, I'm not used to the big city," Jonas said, and the man smiled.

"You don't look it. We've had Amish in here before – *rumspringa* is it, you call it? They find their way in here from the bus station, looking like a fish out of water. You'll soon get used to it, though," he said.

Jonas ordered a slice of red velvet cake. It felt strange to be on his own like this, away from everything familiar. The sense of freedom was palpable, even as Jonas knew he had a job to do. Having settled his bill and thanked the waiter for his help, Jonas left the café, armed with his map and directions. It would not take long to walk to Pine Street, and as he made his way along the busy streets, he wondered what he would say when he got there.

She's going to be surprised to see me, Jonas thought to himself, and he hoped it was a pleasant surprise.

He passed large stores and restaurants, the hustle and bustle of the city going on around him. The air was strange and the noise constant – it was like nothing he had ever seen before. Faith's Creek seemed like a million miles away from this, and when he came to the corner of Pine Street, he looked up at the tenement building above, wondering what to do next. He was at the point where the city changed. The taller blocks of the center were gradually decreasing in height, replaced by lower tenements, some of them done up, others falling into ruin. The stores on the street were different, too. Gone was the glitz and glamor of the fashionable part of town, replaced by practical offerings – a hardware store, a store selling second-hand electricals, and a scruffy-looking launderette next door to a thrift emporium.

"142... this is 190, I suppose it's this way," Jonas said to himself, counting the numbers as he walked up the even side of the street, passing the doors of various tenements, and glancing up above at balconies, where washing was hanging precariously on lines stretched across to the buildings opposite.

142 was a red brick building next to a parking lot. It was five stories high, with an arched entrance that had perhaps once led into a grand building, though the tenement was now severely in decline. Weeds were growing

through cracks in the sidewalk outside, and a homeless man was sitting wrapped in a blanket on the steps. Jonas looked up at the windows above, wondering which one belong to Eve and Jack. It pained him to think of her living somewhere like this. Eve's aunt's house in Faith's Creek was surrounded by a pretty garden with a large vegetable patch. Here, there were only weeds. Jonas checked the listing by the bell, where an intercom would connect him to Eve's apartment. Jack's surname was Simmons, and there was the name next to apartment ten.

"Maybe I should wait until tomorrow. She can't come back with me tonight. If she comes back with me..." Jonas told himself.

He knew he was talking himself out of it, and even as he did so, Jonas felt a sense of guilt. He had come to Philadelphia to help Eve, and now he was backing out at the last minute. He stepped back down the steps, gazing up at the apartment building, and trying to work out which one was number ten. He had just narrowed it down to one of two possibilities when the door to the apartment opened, and Jack Simmons himself appeared.

Jonas had caught a glimpse of him from the flower store window, but Jack did not know Jonas. The man was busy typing into a cell phone, ignoring Jonas as he passed. Jonas knew he now had a chance to speak to Eve alone, but something about Jack made him suspicious. Glancing at the apartment, and back at Jack's retreating back, he made a decision, and so he followed him. The street was busy, but not too busy and he kept at a safe distance. There was something sneaky about the man and he was eager to know more about him and what he was doing. Perhaps, he wanted to know if he was worthy; after all, this was the man who had taken Eve away from everything she knew and brought her to a place such as this.

CHAPTER TWENTY

"**O**h, Esau, please stop crying," Eve said, as she held the *boppli* in her arms, carrying him up and down the apartment lounge.

But Esau would not stop crying, and Eve felt a sense of despair as she looked around her new *home*. The apartment was the one Jack had rented when she had first known him. It was hardly a suitable place to raise a *kinner*. The paint was peeling from the walls, the carpets were dirty, the kitchen had not been updated in years, and the whole family was confined to a single room and the lounge, where windows looked out onto the street below. Eve turned on the television, hoping the noise might distract Esau from his crying. But it only served to make matters worse, so she turned it off again, and sat down on the couch, cradling Esau in her arms.

"I was wrong to come here, wasn't I?" she told herself.

The doubts had been there from the moment she had stepped onto the Greyhound bus. Jack had promised a great deal, but he was yet to deliver it.

"We'll save a deposit for a new place," he had told her, but since they had returned to Philadelphia, he had become cold and distant.

Eve did not understand it. Jack had been so adamant about wanting her back, and about being a *daed* to Esau. But since their return, he had barely spent any time with either of them. He was always out, and Eve did not know where he went, only that he would demand his meals when he returned, before making an excuse and going out again. She had begun to prepare buttered noodles for them – money was tight, and Eve did not know how they could expect to survive the coming months if Jack's prospects did not pick up, or she did not get a job. But with Esau to look after, the prospect of employment seemed uncertain, and Eve was becoming ever more despondent.

"I don't know what your *daed* wants, Esau, but I don't think it's us," Eve said, stroking Esau's head, as the *boppli* finally stopped crying.

She had been putting off writing to Annie since their return. She had nothing *gut* to say, and unless she lied, she knew her cousin-in-law would know something was wrong. Faith's Creek seemed a million miles away from Philadelphia, almost like a dream. The Bible Annie had given her sat on the table next to the couch, and Eve opened it.

"I hereby command you: Be strong and courageous; do not be frightened or dismayed, for the Lord your God is with you wherever you go," Eve read.

It was one of her favorite passages, from the Book of Joshua, and it had been Bishop Beiler who first told her of it during her instruction in the *Ordnung*.

"Gott never leaves you, Eve," the bishop had told her, and Eve believed that with all her heart.

She took comfort in that knowledge, even as she felt far from her faith and those who had supported her. Eve felt guilty for having left Annie and the others behind. She owed them so much, and yet she had wanted to give Jack a chance to prove himself a changed man, she wanted her *boppli* to have a family, a proper one.

Only a few days had passed since she had left Faith's Creek, and already Eve realized Jack had not changed at all. He was the same man she had known before, and Eve was angry with herself for allowing her residual feelings to have influenced her. He had expected her to move straight back into his bed, but she had resisted, saying that he needed to win her back. That had made him angry and for a moment, she thought he might strike her, instead, he had left. Maybe that was why he was so distant, but she needed time, and now she knew she had made the wrong decision.

"Why did I do it?" she asked herself, as a footfall on the landing announced Jack's return.

The door opened, and Jack appeared, looking around him expectantly.

"Haven't you got dinner started yet?" he asked, sitting down with a sigh on the couch next to her.

"I was just going to make buttered noodles. Is that all right?" Eve asked.

Jack turned his nose up. "We're not in Faith's Creek anymore, Eve. I'm not Amish. I'm not eating Amish food. Go out and get something from the store – macaroni and cheese, something like that," he said.

Eve did not know where she would find the money for a different meal, but she rose to her feet, carrying Esau in her arms, even as Jack made no attempt to help.

"Will you watch Esau whilst I go?" she asked.

Jack shook his head. "I'm tired, Eve. I've been out all afternoon. Is it really too much to expect his own mother to watch him?" Jack asked.

Eve was taken aback at these words. It was as though Jack had decided he wanted nothing to do with Esau, even as he had said all the right things in Faith's Creek. Eve was starting to suspect he had only wanted her there to do precisely this – to cook, clean, and look after him. He did not want a wife, and he did not want to be a *daed* to his son. It all made sense now. A leopard did not change its spots, and Jack was just the same as he had always been. Eve felt a fool for having trusted him, even as she despaired at the prospect of ever being rid of him. She had made her bed and now she had to lie in it.

"I'll take him with me then," Eve said, pulling her shawl around her shoulders.

"Don't be long. I'm hungry. Isn't there anything to eat all?" Jack demanded.

"Peanuts, that's it," Eve said, pointing to a packet on the counter.

Jack groaned, but Eve was not about to argue. She hurried out of the apartment, taking the stairwell, for she did not trust the lift to work properly. The tenement was a grim place, and Eve felt fearful walking on her own. The stairwell was dark, and at one point, Eve could hear sobbing coming from one of the lower apartments. It was a far cry from Faith's Creek, where community meant everything. Here, in the "City of Brotherly Love," she had found only a cold welcome – nothing like that she had received in Faith's Creek. Esau was crying again, and in the lobby of the tenement building, Eve struggled with him in her arms.

"Oh, Esau, can't you stop crying? I feel like crying, too, but we've got to make the best of it. We're here now, and that's that," Eve said, sighing, as she pulled her shawl around her and pulled open the door onto the steps leading down to the street.

The homeless man who always seemed to sit there was hunched up in a blanket, and Eve stepped to one side, fearful of what he might do. But as she did so, a figure stepped out in front of her, and to her amazement, Eve came face to face with Jonas. For a moment, she stared at him, astonished to see him standing there.

"Eve, I'm so glad to see you," he said.

Eve's eyes grew wide with astonishment and her heart fluttered in her chest. She wanted to walk into his arms, but knew it was wrong; after all, she hardly knew him. But, Jonas was not meant to be in Philadelphia. He should be in Faith's Creek – what was he doing here?

"I... Jonas? What are you doing here?" she asked.

Jonas looked suddenly embarrassed. "I wanted to talk to you. I'm sorry, maybe I shouldn't have come," he said, taking a step back.

Eve came down the steps toward him. "But you didn't come all this way to run away. I don't understand why you're here. I'm sorry about the other night. I shouldn't have left as I did. But those awful women made me so upset," Eve said, thinking back to the board games evening.

Jonas shook his head. "You've done nothing wrong. It's me that needs to apologize. I should've stood up for you against Lydia Backwater. I shouldn't have let you leave like that. I'm so sorry. I didn't want you to think I felt the same way as her or the others. I don't," he said.

Eve was somewhat taken aback – he had come all the way from Faith's Creek to tell her that? Eve had felt guilty for the way she had treated him. She had accepted his invitation to the board games evening, knowing full well what such an invitation meant, even as she was contemplating a return to Philadelphia with Jack. It had been a terrible thing to do, and she had known just how much it would upset him.

"I know you don't, and it's... so sweet of you to come here and tell me that. I'm sorry you've come all this way, though. You shouldn't have. It can't have been easy getting here, and... have you got somewhere to stay?" she asked.

Jonas shook his head. "It doesn't matter. I'll find somewhere. I wanted to come. I wanted to tell you how I felt," he replied.

Eve's heart skipped a beat – what did this mean? Things happened differently in Amish communities. Kind words between a man and a woman could soon blossom into something more. But Eve barely knew Jonas, as much as she felt flattered by his appearance and the fact that he had made such a journey to see her.

"How you felt?" she asked.

He nodded. "I thought... well, I don't know... I really enjoyed getting to know you back home, and I was confused when you left like this. Why did you come back here? Was it because of what Lydia and the others said?" he asked.

It was a question Eve could not answer, even though she had thought she knew what she was doing. Returning to Philadelphia had been meant as a return to the familiar. She had believed Jack had changed, but just a short time in the big city had shown her that was not the case. Nothing had changed – if anything, things had got worse. A seedy tenement in an unpleasant downtown district was no place to raise a *kinner*. Esau could not grow up here, and not with a *daed* who did not care about him or want to know him.

"I left because... I didn't think I was welcome, if that's what you mean. But not by everyone – the Quilting circle was kind. The bishop and Sarah, the stallholders, my aunt and cousin and Annie... were all wonderful... actually, most people were kind. Kinder than I ever expected them to be. But the ones who shouted... shouted loudly. I didn't feel welcome, not at all," Eve said, thinking back to the barbed comments and sideways glances and realizing that she hadn't run to Jack, she had run away from the hurt.

But in Philadelphia, there was no welcome – not from anyone. Eve had no friends, only Jack, and he had proved to be just his old familiar self. How easily she had fallen for his words, only to have her dreams dashed once again.

"They're just fools, Eve. They don't know what they're talking about. I've had a lifetime of my Aunt Alima giving her opinions on everything. She's only happy when she's complaining," Jack said.

Eve could not help but smile. "She certainly gave her opinion on me," she replied, shaking her head.

"And are you going to let her scare you away? Why not stand up to her? She's just a bully, Eve. You're worth so much more than this; than what he's led you back to," Jonas said, looking at Eve beseechingly.

Eve was grateful to him. He was proving himself to be worth ten of Jack, even as Eve did not know what to say or do in response. Was he asking her to go back to Faith's Creek and be with him? She had thought so much about what was best for Esau, and she had truly believed he would be better off with both a *mamm* and a *daed*, and yet now they had returned to Philadelphia, Jack had proved himself the very opposite of what he should have been.

"I don't know... what are you saying, Jonas?" she asked.

Jonas took a deep breath, glancing up towards the apartment with an angry expression on his face.

"He's got another woman, Eve. I've seen her. I followed him," he replied.

CHAPTER TWENTY-ONE

Eve was shocked, even though she was not surprised. Jack had promised her he had eyes only for her, but his behavior since their return to Philadelphia had been decidedly odd – he had been out at all hours, making excuses to leave, and coming home without telling her where he had been. She had been suspicious, but she had tried her best to give Jack the benefit of the doubt. He had promised her a new start – for them all – and she had trusted him to keep his word. But in truth, Eve knew nothing of what Jack had been doing since she had left Philadelphia all those months ago. Back then, he had taken up with another woman, and despite his assurances to the contrary, it seemed that the woman had remained a feature in his life.

"I... you saw him?" Eve asked.

Jonas nodded. "He came out of here earlier. I know I shouldn't have done it, but I followed him to a tenement like this, a few blocks away. I could see through the window. There was a woman, and... she had a *boppli*, too," Jonas said.

Eve gasped. Jonas had no reason to lie. He had come to Philadelphia to help her, and now he was telling her something that was both shocking and yet entirely believable. She shook her head, hardly able to comprehend what Jonas was saying, even as the revelation made perfect sense.

"A *boppli*... but, he can't have. I won't... *nee*, but... it makes sense," she said, as much to herself as to Jonas.

"I'm so sorry, Eve. I didn't want to tell you this. I wanted what was best for you. I hoped you'd prayed about this and come back to Philadelphia because you believed you could make things work with Jack. I didn't want to stand in your way, but I wanted you to know I don't feel the same as those women, and so many others don't either. We want you and Esau to be a part of our community, to learn the *Ordnung*, and to make a commitment. You'll be supported – you've got so many friends in Faith's Creek, Eve. You've got me, for a start," Jonas said.

Eve gave a weak smile. She still could not entirely take it in. It was simply astonishing to think of the lies Jack had told her. Would she ever have discovered the truth if Jonas had not told her?

"You've proved yourself the dearest of friends, Jonas," Eve said, just as Esau began to cry.

"I hope I haven't overstepped the mark. But I had to tell you what I saw. I couldn't let you live like this without knowing the truth. But it's got to be your decision," Jonas said.

Eve sighed. She had prayed so hard, and she had truly believed she was doing the right thing. But some words of Bishop Beiler's now came back to her.

"*Gott* doesn't always lead us in straight lines. Sometimes, we need a diversion or two to make sense of things, and sometimes we take those diversions ourselves, without listening. We don't always get it right, but *Gott* knows the way," he had said, and now Eve began to understand.

She had left Faith's Creek with the sincere belief she was doing the right thing. But her decision had been rushed, and she had used the cruel words of her detractors as a catalyst. Jack's offer had come at just the right time, and his assurances of having turned over a new leaf had seemed sincere. The reality was very different, and now, in her heart of hearts, Eve knew she should never have left her new familiarity behind. Philadelphia was not her home. It had never been her home. Her parents had taken her away from Faith's Creek when she was very young, and they had brought her up to believe she had freedom away from the community she was supposed to know. But that apparent freedom had only led to heartache, and the revelation of Jack's other life was the final straw.

"I've been such a fool," Eve whispered.

Jonas shook his head, reaching out and placing his hand on her arm. "You've not been a fool, Eve, not at all. You weren't to know he hadn't changed his ways. You came here in good faith, believing he wanted a family, but..." Jonas began, but he was interrupted by the opening of the tenement door, and a shout from behind.

"Eve?" Jack shouted.

Eve turned to find him standing at the top of the steps, looking at her impatiently.

"Jack, I..." she began, but again, he interrupted her.

"Weren't you going to the store? How long does it take? I've been out all day, I'm hungry, and all you're planning to give me is a bowl of those disgusting buttered noodles. I'll get a pizza or something," he said, storming down the steps, and without any sense of having recognized Jonas' presence.

"Jack, you stop right there. I'll not be spoken to like that. I know where you've been. You've been with that other woman, haven't you? And your other baby," Eve said.

Jack turned to her in astonishment, his eyes growing wide. He had the look of a man who knows he has been caught, and that there is nothing he can do or say to escape his entrapment.

"I saw you, Jack. I saw you with that other woman," Jonas said.

Jack looked at him angrily. "Who are you?" he demanded.

"This is Jonas. He's come all the way from Faith's Creek – he told me what you've done. Don't deny it, Jack. You haven't changed a bit, have you?" Eve exclaimed.

She was growing angry now – angry with Jack, and angry with herself for not seeing through his lies. He had seemed so sincere, but it had all been a front. He had lied to her, and for what? So he could have a housekeeper whilst he tended to his other family? Eve felt humiliated, and she shook her head, wondering what to do next.

"I... it's not like that, Eve. It's not," Jack said, but he did not deny it, nor did he fight for her.

He did not tell her he loved her, nor express his desire for her to stay.

"Then what is it like, Jack? What is it?" Eve asked, fixing him with a defiant gaze.

"He shouldn't have been spying on me. Why did he come here?" Jack demanded, turning on Jonas, who stood his ground.

He was a tall man, well-built, and fit from working on the farm, he was more than a match for Jack should the city dweller choose to pick a fight.

"He came here to remind me what really matters, and to let me know that I have friends who do miss me. This isn't me. I shouldn't ever have listened to you. But that's you all over, isn't it, Jack? You think you can say the right things and be believed. I was a fool to think it, but I'm not going to make that mistake again. I don't love you, Jack. I thought you'd changed, I thought I could feel the way I did before. But I can't. I was a fool then, and I'm a fool now." Eve was trembling with anger, and Esau began to cry, no doubt sensing her stress. She shushed him, holding him protectively in her arms, as Jack seethed in front of her.

"So you're going to go back to being brainwashed, are you? Back to your cult?" he said, but before Eve could reply, Jonas had stepped between them.

"If you think decent people living good, Christian lives are brainwashed, then it's you that needs help. We choose our way of life, and we choose it joyfully. The problem with people like you is your closed mind. You think you're so enlightened, surrounded by technology and gadgets, living in a big city, with every convenience at your disposal. Maybe it has its attractions for a while. But I pity you – no community, no family, no sense of meaning or purpose. We have all that and more in Faith's Creek, and we want to welcome Eve and Esau home," he said.

Jack was lost for words, and he shook his head, scowling at Eve, who felt tears rising in her eyes. Jonas was right – the world of Philadelphia, with its bright lights and bustle, seemed attractive. It promised so much, and yet delivered only heartache and a feeling of emptiness. Eve had been happy in Faith's Creek – not because she had a lot of things or dressed in fancy clothes, but because she had known kindness and friendship. She had been surrounded by faith, hope, and love – these were the hallmarks of a *gut* life, and it was a life she wanted desperately to return to.

"*Denke*," she whispered, and Jonas turned to her and smiled.

"You don't have to stay here," he said.

Eve glanced at Jack – he was pitiable. She had been blinded by his false promises and the misguided thought of giving Esau a family at any cost. Her own happiness had been forgotten, and Eve had forgotten where that happiness lay – in Faith's Creek, with those who loved her. But a family was not what she had gained in moving to Philadelphia – she had lost it, and now she longed for it.

"I don't want to," she said.

"He's still my son," Jack exclaimed, looking up at Eve and pointing his finger at her.

"And I'm sure we can work out a way for you to see him when you want to. But it's me that's taken care of him all this time. You didn't want anything to do with him, and you're not going to take him away from me," Eve replied.

Jack knew nothing about her having abandoned Esau in the flower store, but Eve knew he would use it against her if he did. He would claim she was unfit to be Esau's *mamm*, and that custody was questionable. It was a risk, she knew, but she was determined to stand her ground.

"We'll see about that," he snarled.

"And I'm sure the courts would be glad to hear of your double life," Jonas said.

"Get your things and leave, if that's what you want," Jack replied, and turning on his heels, he stormed off along the street, shouting threats as he went.

"It's all right, I don't think he'll trouble you any longer," Jonas said.

Eve breathed a sigh of relief, even as she felt overwhelmed by what had just happened.

"I... I can't thank you enough," she said.

Jonas smiled at her. "You don't have to thank me, not at all. I did what I did because... well, you mean a lot to me, Eve. I know we don't know one another that well. But that afternoon by the creek... it really meant something to me. I was really looking forward to getting to know you better, and when you left for Philadelphia... I was really upset. I had to come and tell you – I had to tell you we want you back," he said.

Eve smiled. "And I want to come back. I couldn't think of anywhere else I'd rather be than in Faith's Creek, with all my friends, and my new friend, too... I want to get to know you better, Jonas. And I think Esau does, too," Eve said, glancing down at the *boppli*, who was reaching out toward Jonas and gurgling, a big smile on his face.

Jonas smiled, and he reached out his arms, taking Esau and smiling down at him.

"I can wait here whilst you get your things. I know it's late, but we can get the Greyhound bus back to Faith's Creek overnight... if you like," he said.

Eve nodded. Her mind was made up. She could not remain in Philadelphia a moment longer. Her life was no longer there. She belonged in Faith's Creek, surrounded by her friends and family, and now, Jonas...

"I'll get my things. I can't thank you enough, Jonas," she said, but Jonas shook his head.

"You don't need to thank me. I came because... I believed I should. I felt as though *Gott* was calling me to it, leading me. I prayed about it. I knew I had to come," Jonas said.

Eve smiled. "And now you're here, I know it was meant to be," she replied, and smiling at him, she hurried back into the tenement building to collect her things, glad to be leaving Philadelphia – and Jack – behind.

CHAPTER TWENTY-TWO

The ride back to Faith's Creek on the Greyhound bus was uneventful. Eve fell asleep on Jonas's shoulder, and she awoke in the early hours, just as the dawn was breaking.

"We're nearly back," Jonas said, smiling down at her.

"Oh, I'm sorry, I didn't mean to sleep the whole time," Eve said, yawning and sitting up.

Esau was asleep in her arms, and for a moment she felt embarrassed at having rested her head on Jonas's shoulder. But she remembered his words about friendship – and something more – and as the bus trundled to a stop, he helped her up, carrying her bag, and his own, as they stepped off the bus. It had only been a few days since

Eve had left Faith's Creek, but it seemed to her as though a lifetime had passed. What would her aunt say when she arrived back home? Would her family be angry with her? Eve felt nervous, even though she knew she was doing the right thing.

"Will you come with me? To my aunt's house, I mean," Eve asked.

Jonas nodded. "I'd be glad to," he said, offering her his arm.

It felt natural to take it, and Eve was only too glad to have Jonas at her side. He had already done so much for her, and if it had not been for him, her life would surely have continued in the same miserable fashion for years to come, part of a double life, created by a man who did not love her.

"I wonder what they'll say. I hope they won't be angry with me," Eve said, as they walked together along the road leading between the cornfields in the direction of Faith's Creek.

"I spoke to Annie before I came. She gave me the address. I think they'll just be pleased to have you back," Jonas replied.

"Annie gave me her Bible before I left. It was so kind of her. She wanted me to keep reading it, and studying the *Ordnung*, too. I'm ready to commit. I suppose I've had my own kind of *rumspringa*, and I know where I want to be," Eve said, shaking her head.

"I never had a *rumspringa*. There was always so much to do on the farm. But after a day spent in Philadelphia... I'm glad to be back in Faith's Creek. I can hear myself think again," Jonas said.

He was right. There was peace and tranquility here, and Eve, too, knew how much she had missed it. They had come to the gate of her aunt's house now, and to Eve's surprise, Doctor Yoder appeared at the door.

"How did you know? It's only just happened. They were just saying they needed to contact you," he said.

Eve looked at the doctor in confusion and felt panic well up inside of her. "I... I don't understand. What's happened?" she asked.

The doctor smiled. "It's Annie. She's given birth to a beautiful little girl. Go in, it's all over now, she's sitting up with her in a chair in the parlor," he said.

Eve relaxed and they rushed forward, and up the steps.

As they entered the house, Linda turned to Eve in astonishment, and Annie looked up from her chair by the stove. Marshall was leaning at her side, and in her arms was the newborn *boppli*, fast asleep.

"Eve... what happened? How did you know?" Annie exclaimed.

Eve glanced at Jonas. "It's a long story. But I'm so glad to be home... if that is okay?" she replied.

Linda pulled her into her arms and held her close, patting her back. "It is wonderful news, we are so glad to see you. It looks like a double celebration is in order."

"*Denke,* and congratulations, Annie."

EPILOGUE

The following days passed in something of a blur. Eve's fears about returning were unfounded, and her family welcomed her with open arms. They were shocked to hear what Jack had done, and Eve explained how it was Jonas who had discovered the truth. He was the hero of the hour, and despite the new arrival, Linda insisted he come for dinner with them by way of saying *denke*. Eve was only too pleased to issue the invitation, and three nights later, Jonas came to join the family for dinner.

"It's a beautiful name – Miriam," Jonas said, as Eve's aunt served out bowls of buttered noodles.

"It was my great aunt's. I thought it was lovely, and that's how it came about. Matthew was the alternative if we had a boy. I know most *mamm's* expect one or the other, but I could never decide and I didn't care. It was just so wonderful when Doctor Yoder told me and handed me the precious little bundle," Annie said, glancing over at the crib, where the *boppli* was fast asleep.

Esau was going to be delighted to have a little cousin when he got used to her. Right now, Eve was holding him in her arms, and the whole family gathered around the table. She could not have felt happier to be home, surrounded by the people she loved.

"I think Esau's still a little suspicious of a new person who looks like him, but smaller," Eve said, and Annie laughed.

"I think they'll grow up to be the best of friends, don't you?" she asked.

Eve nodded. "I know they will," she said, glancing at Jonas, who smiled.

"Which means, you've got to stick around, Eve. *Nee* more bright city lights for you," Annie said.

"*Jah, nee* more, you gave us all quite a scare and we are glad to have you home," Marshall said.

"Don't worry, I won't be going anywhere, from now on," Eve replied.

Her mind was made up, and her prayers were answered. *Gott* had shown her the way, even as she had thought she knew best. Looking back over the past few weeks, she could see *Gott's* gentle hand guiding her along the right path.

"We're glad to hear it," Marshall said.

"And what about you, Jonas? What's next for you?" Linda asked.

Jonas sighed and put down his fork. "Things are still difficult at the farm. My brother won't pull his weight – and I'm not betraying any confidences in saying that, but I wish he'd learn to offer some help now and then. He's talking about leaving Faith's Creek. But I don't think he'll like the outside world quite as much as he thinks. I know I don't," Jonas replied.

"I'm sure he'll step up to the mark when it comes to it. But you and Henry do a *gut* job up there, Jonas. Don't ever let anyone say differently," Marshall said.

Jonas smiled. "It's *gut*, honest work, and I'm grateful for it, but it is too much for us. Maybe, I will take on some help. I think I let things get on top of me when there is always a way. If my brother doesn't want the work, someone else will."

"That sounds like a *gut* plan," Marshall said, "I may know someone who could help."

"*Denke*. My *mamm's* getting better, too. Doctor Yoder came to see her this morning. She's regaining her strength," he said.

"That's wonderful news, Jonas," Annie said.

Miriam began to cry, waking Esau from his sleep, and Eve rose from the table, beckoning Jonas to follow her.

"Let's step outside. We'll never get them both quiet if they're together," she said, and Jonas followed her out onto the porch.

It was a beautiful evening, the sun casting long shadows across the garden. Marshall's vegetable garden was coming into its own, and the flowers Annie grew were blossoming in the beds surrounding it.

"I never really appreciated how important green space is, and look at that view across the cornfields, isn't it beautiful?" Eve said, cradling Esau in her arms.

He had fallen back to sleep now, his head lolled to the side, and his thumb in his mouth.

Jonas nodded. "I never tire of it. It's not easy getting up to milk in the winter, but when the days are long, I can't think of anything more beautiful than seeing the sunrise over Faith's Creek. It's like *Gott* gives us another chance, a new start each day," Jonas replied.

Eve nodded. She was glad to have been given a new start, and now she wanted only to look to the future and see the *gut* things to come.

"You believe in second chances then?" she asked.

Jonas nodded. "We all deserve second chances. Like my brother, Levi. He's not a bad person, he's just lost his way. If he steps up, I'll give him another chance. We'd all like to think others would give us a second chance, too – that's why we've got to be willing to give them ourselves," he replied.

It seemed so simple when put like that, even as Eve wondered what certain others would think of her return.

"Do you think I can become part of this community?" she asked.

He nodded. "*Jah*, but you must believe in it with your whole heart, can you do that?" he asked.

This was the question. The moment of commitment. To study the *Ordnung* was one thing, but to embrace the community as her own was another. To commit to the faith and to this way of life, meant doing so with her whole heart, and now Eve nodded, smiling at Jonas who reached out and took her hand in his.

"I do," she replied, and as she spoke those words, it felt to Eve as though the burdens of the past had disappeared.

She was no longer a stranger or an outsider looking in. Eve had come to Faith's Creek knowing nothing of the future. She had intended to abandon Esau and flee. But something had kept her there – a seed planted through kindness and compassion. That seed had grown, nurtured by those around her, and now it felt as though the blossom had come, and Eve's faith was revealed in all its glory.

"I'm so glad to hear you say that. It has to be your decision and yours alone. It can't be anyone else's. You're making a commitment, and that means something – for you, and the community," he said.

Eve smiled. "It's the right time to do it. I've come home. I realize that now," she said, leaning down and kissing Esau on the forehead.

"And... do you think you can give me a second chance, too?" Jonas asked.

Eve did not need to think twice. Jonas did not need to ask such a question. It was she who needed a second chance, and now she smiled at him and nodded.

"You don't need a second chance. It's me that doesn't deserve it, but I know you don't see it like that. You came after me, Jonas. You believed in me, and if you still can, I'll stay, and I'll face whatever criticism I get. I'm proud to be part of this community, I'm proud of Esau, and I'm proud of what's to come – with you," she said.

Jonas smiled at her, a look of relief coming over his face.

"I... I wasn't sure. I didn't know if you'd find it all a bit much," he said.

Eve shook her head. "It's me that comes with a past, Jonas. I've got Esau to think about, but, if you're happy to have a *boppli* in tow, then..." she began.

Jonas leaned forward and kissed her. The kiss filled her with warmth and joy in a way she had never felt before.

As their lips parted, he smiled at her again.

"I love you and I'll love Esau like he's my own, and I'll support you all the way – in your commitment to the faith, in taking care of Esau, and running the flower store now Annie's had the *boppli*. I'll be here for you," he said.

Eve nodded, as tears welled up in her eyes.

"I love you too. All I've ever wanted is to belong – and now I do," she said, and leaning forward, she kissed him once again, feeling happier than she had ever thought possible, and knowing just where her future lay.

* * *

If you enjoyed this book you will love A Love to Heal her Heart

AMISH OF FAITH'S CREEK 4 BOOK BOX SET – PREVIEW

* * *

"I have told you these things,
so that in me you may have peace.
In this world you will have trouble.
But take heart!
I have overcome the world."
- John 16:3

* * *

A cool breeze lifted the ties of her bonnet and let them fall gently against her neck. Roseanna Wagler brushed the tie away absently and closed her eyes. The breeze felt good and clean with the scent of grass as she moved through the field. It eased the weight from her shoulders and cooled the sweat on her brow. Today was a perfect day to be working in the meadow. The sort of day she lived for and there was plenty of work to be done.

Opening her eyes, she glanced across the land. How she loved this view. The vista of green spread out before her like *Gott's* perfect patchwork. There were fields of grass, dotted with black and white Friesian cattle. As she watched, she could almost smell their earthy scent and hear their moos as they came in for milking.

Her eyes moved across to the horses, bays, the occasional gray, and the big chestnut Dutch horses that the landscape and the Amish were famous for. Then there were the beautiful mixed colors of corn spread out before her along with all varieties of potatoes, vegetables, and the river in the distance. It was perfect, peaceful, and filled her with joy and only a touch of loneliness.

Wiggling her bare toes in the earth she lowered her head and looked at their own fields. It was good fertile soil and the crop would be heavy this year. The barley was not quite turning. The ears were still upright and the color still green. As it ripened the nutty scent would increase, but for now, it was sweet and barely detectable. This was the ideal time to walk between the rows to pluck out the weeds. So why was she feeling guilty?

The sound of hooves traveling on gravel carried across the field and her eyes were drawn to the buggy. The horse was trotting fast. It looked like *Daed* was worried. Maybe she should have gone with them. Roseanna's hand reached down and wrapped around the wild oats. With a quick pull, she ripped out the weed and placed it in her basket while walking along the row without needing to look. Up ahead a large patch of weeds was choking the barley.

No, she was right to stay.

The work needed doing and *bopplis* were born every day. There was nothing special about this birth. Nothing that needed her to be there more than she was needed in the fields. It promised to be a good crop. To provide them with an income to keep up with the rent and tide them over the winter. It would be careless to leave it unattended just to visit with her sister-in-law. Just to take her to the hospital. Anyway, the buggy would be crowded enough.

Quickly her hands reached for another weed as her eyes followed the buggy. It was fading into the distance now and the pace had not slowed. In fact, she couldn't be sure at this distance, but she thought the horse was cantering. A hand seemed to clench onto her gut and squeeze the air from her lungs.

Should she have gone?

Mary would be fine. So why did she worry? Her brother already had one child and Mary had shown no problems throughout this pregnancy. Yet *Daed* had been different this morning. Something about the look in his eyes made Rose wonder if she should have gone with them. Absently she reached for the weeds and plucked them from the field. *Gott* would take care of her family. He would see that all was right with the world. The way He sent the rain and the sunshine... but what about the weeds? He sent those too and without help, they would swamp the fields and smother the barley. If she did not tend the field, the harvest would be poor. Maybe it was the same with *kinner*. If you did not attend the birth, then things got out of hand. But her brother, David was there with her *daed*. They did not need her.

From across the field, the sound of a young girls' laughter floated on the breeze. Katie could always find something to laugh at. Right now she would be tending to Atlee, her brother's and Mary's two-year-old son. As another peel of laughter floated towards her, guilt flooded her stomach with bile. Katie was only eleven and yet she had taken it upon herself to look after Atlee. Rose ripped at the weeds, pulling them out as fast as she could and trying to blot out the thought of her sister doing all the work. No, that was wrong. Katie and her twin Lydia did the majority of the housework, the cooking, cleaning, and washing. They baked and roasted and kept the house as clean as it had been before their *mamm* deserted them. But they never milked the cow or chopped wood. They never plowed the fields or harvested the corn. Rose did those so her sisters didn't have to. She took on more of the farm as her *daed* got older. It had never been a burden. Reach and pull, reach and pull. The weeds grasped onto the dry soil and each time it seemed harder to pull them loose. It was as if they were fighting her. As if they defied her and wanted her to know she should not be here.

A cry rang across the field and Rose stopped. The sound of a child in pain filled her with despair. It took her back to the day their mother left. The sound of her sister's crying still haunted her dreams... almost as much as the look in her *daed's* eyes. Katie and Lydia were just six years old. Roseanna had been fifteen, almost an adult, and it had fallen on her to become the woman of the house.

A cut formed on her hand as it slipped across a ryegrass stalk. The weed seemed to wave before her, defiantly happy that it managed to draw blood. She bent down and wrapped her fingers around it pulling once more. For a second the tough grass held firm and tears formed in her eyes. How could she go on? Then the grass came loose and she almost fell backward.

This was her place. The crying from the field's headland had stopped. As always Katie had eased the child's tears. Now she would be bouncing little Atlee on her knee. Cooing and chuckling with him. Making him forget his *mamm* was not there. It had been just the same when their *mamm* left. Katie had taken over. She had looked after so much even though she was so young. She had held her sisters and soothed away their tears. While they clung to her, her little face filled with resolve as she dried her tears, Rose had felt so awkward. It should have been her doing those things but she didn't feel like an adult. All she wanted to do was drop to her knees and let Katie hold her. Then she had fled to the stables and watched the horses and the chickens. They had no worries, no stresses and they went about their day as if *Gott* provided everything for them. It had been a hard lesson. To know that she had to *let go and let Gott,* but she could not do it. On the outside, she carried on, but inside she was betrayed and hurt and she wanted to scream at *Gott* that it was not fair.

Gradually the years passed, but she never got over the hurt. It was like armor and she wore it to protect her from getting too close. If you let no one in, no one could betray you.

All the time Katie had been so small and yet so in control. Instead of crying, she helped others. At first, Rose thought of her as a child playing house but that changed. Soon she was so proficient. In a few years, she had taken over the cooking from Rose. Their meals had changed from burnt offerings to good, healthy, and tasty food. Rose had fled the house and found solace on the farm. The work was hard and yet easier... for her at least. It stopped her thinking, stopped her worrying, and kept her busy. There was no need to worry about anyone else when she worked the fields. No need to worry who she would hurt, or who would leave, or anything like that. The work just was, and she was out in *Gott's* glorious sunshine.

"You need to marry," *Daed* had said just last week.

Rose had nodded and told him she would see, but no *mann* had asked to drive her home from service in over a year. No *mann* wanted a woman who could work as hard as he could. They wanted a cook and a cleaner, they wanted someone to bear them children, and Rose could never see herself doing any of those things.

The crying was replaced by laughter, as she knew it would be. Katie was a wonder with children. It was something that always mystified Rose. How did you stop a *boppli* from crying? How could you look after something so fragile and how did you have the patience to put up with so much crying? In all her years she had shied away from *kinner*. Animals were easy to live with... but *kinner*? They were difficult, awkward, and so vulnerable she could not bring herself to even think about having one. Maybe it was because of the hurt.

As she moved along the rows, she thought about the hurt look on her *daed's* face. How he wanted to see her happy and no matter how she tried she couldn't explain that she already was. There was no need for a husband in her life.

For many hours she had prayed on this. It didn't matter nothing came to her. There was no answer to her hurt. Nothing would make her trust. What if she married a *mann* and then changed her mind? What if he changed his mind? What if they had children and she let them down? If she betrayed them as her *mamm* had? No, it was too much to bear, she was much better off as she was. Like this, she could hurt no one. Here, she did her work and talked to *Gott,* her life was just as He wanted. She was sure of it. The loneliness was something everyone felt, she was sure of it.

Grab this wonderful Box Set now for FREE with Kindle Unlimited Amish of Faith's Creek 4 Book Box Set

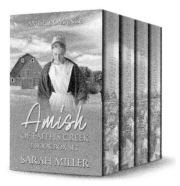

ALSO BY SARAH MILLER

All my books are FREE on Kindle Unlimited

If you love Amish Romance, the sweet, clean stories of Sarah Miller you can receive free stories and join me for the latest news on upcoming books here

These are some of my reader favorites:

The Amish Family and Faith Collection

Amish Baby Hope

5 Amish Brothers Series

Find all Sarah's books on Amazon and click the yellow follow button

This book is dedicated to the wonderful Amish people and the faithful life that they live.

Go in peace, my friends.

As an independent author, Sarah relies on your support. If you enjoyed this book, please leave a review on Amazon or Goodreads.

ABOUT THE AUTHOR

Sarah Miller was born in Pennsylvania and spent her childhood close to the Amish people. Weekends were spent doing chores; quilting or eventually babysitting in the community. She grew up to love their culture and the simple lifestyle and had many Amish friends. The one thing that you can guarantee when you are near the Amish, Sarah believes is that you will feel close to God.

Many years later she married Martin who is the love of her life and moved to England. There she started to write stories about the Amish. Recently after a lot of persuasion from her best friend she has decided to publish her stories. They draw on inspiration from her relationship with the Amish and with God and she hopes you enjoy reading them as much as she did writing them. Many of the stories are based on true events but names have been changed and even though they are authentic at times artistic license has been used.

Sarah likes her stories simple and to hold a message and they help bring her closer to her faith. She currently lives in Yorkshire, England with her husband Martin and seven very spoiled chickens.

She would love to meet you on Facebook at https://www.facebook.com/SarahMillerBooks

Sarah hopes her stories will both entertain and inspire and she wishes that you go with God.